PRAISE

TVA BABY

"Bisson's work is a fresh, imaginative attempt to confront some of the problems of our time. It is the Bissons of the field upon whom the future of science fiction depends."
—*Washington Post Book World*

"With his sharp accuracy and sharp humor, he seems to me the Mark Twain of science fiction."
—Kim Stanley Robinson

"Terry Bisson is one of the sharpest short story writers in science fiction today."
—*Sacramento Book Review*

★ TVA BABY

TVA BABY
and
other stories

TERRY BISSON

PM PRESS
2011
★

ISBN: 978-1-60486-405-2
LCCN: 2010916471

PM Press
P.O. Box 23912
Oakland, CA 94623
pmpress.org

Printed in the USA on recycled paper.

Cover: John Yates/Stealworks.com
Layout: Jonathan Rowland

DEDICATION

for Giles
who put on a shirt his mother made
and went on the air

Contents

TVA Baby

I'm a TVA baby. My father was a Yankee, from Michigan I think, one of those educated engineers who came down here to dam up the rivers and bring electric lights and indoor plumbing to the bedarkened South: FDR's potlatch. Then they all went off to the War and some returned and others didn't. It's Destiny that decides such things.

I fly a lot. I slept through the takeoff from Nashville and woke up just in time to hear the man in the seat next to me say, "There's the Mississippi, Ned."

"Ned," the Ned he was talking to, was a boy of about eight in the window seat. I was in the aisle seat. I looked over them both, out the little oval window, and saw a long lake laid out like a coonskin, running north and south, with skinny legs of muddy water extending east and west.

"That's Kentucky Lake," I said. "Or Barkley, not the Mississippi."

"Excuse me?" he said.

"Kentucky Lake is the Tennessee River," I said, "dammed up by TVA. Barkley Lake is the Cumberland. Both run into the Ohio here, only twenty miles apart. We're still a hundred miles east of the Mississippi."

"Who is he?" asked "Ned," the kid.

"Some nosy A-hole," said the man. He was about forty with a flattop and an Opryland T-shirt.

"I was just trying to be helpful," I said. "You got it wrong. It's against the law to mislead children!" It should be, anyway.

"Can I help?" asked the stewardess. "Please don't shout."

"Sorry," I said. I almost never shout. "I'm a TVA baby. This ignoramus in the middle seat is so ignorant that he thinks Kentucky Lake is the Mississippi River!"

"I am a Lieutenant Commander in the US Navy," he said. "On vacation, and I do believe I know a lake from a river."

"I can see how one could make that mistake," I said. Though I couldn't help adding: "Though I am dismayed to learn that a U.S. naval officer could be so ignorant as to the geographic layout of the country he is supposedly supposed to defend."

"Don't pay any attention to him, Ned," the man said. "He's crazy."

I hear that a lot. I wanted to kill him. I usually carry a gun for just such occasions, but they are no longer allowed on commercial flights, so I rammed the heel of my hand upward, into his nose and drove the bone into his brain, such as it was.

Well, then, all hell broke loose. So to speak. First of all, there was the blood; you hardly ever see blood on a commercial flight. And then he was making this honking noise, trying to breathe and spraying blood all over the magazines in the seat pocket, and the back of the seat as well. Then he jerked once and died, but it was too late. All the other passengers were standing up, trying to get out of their seats, which are all jammed together, economy class wise, so it was like a little mini-riot. And here was the stewardess, excuse me, flight attendant, back again.

"Sir, sir," she was saying, meaning, of course, me. One only gets called "sir" by cops and such, so I got alarmed. Sure enough, there was a big guy behind me, trying to grab my arms and waving plastic handcuffs.

You can imagine the chaos. I figured it was time to split. The big guy wasn't so big with a fork in his carotid; even a plastic fork will do if you know how to wield it. I jammed him face down between the seats to bleed out and grabbed the gun out his ankle holster, and there's nothing like a gun, even a little one, to cool things out. It's like waving a magic wand. Everybody got real quiet.

Even the kid was quiet. The "Ned." He was watching me like a hawk or maybe an owl, all owl-eyed.

The gun was a big help. I used it to direct the attendant to the back of the plane. The aisle was clear. Everybody was sitting down again, watching me. I stopped on the way to get my carry-on out of the overhead.

"Open it," I said, pointing with the gun at the Emergency Exit door. They're good for pointing.

"Not not not allowed," she said with a combination of words and almost illegible (is that the word?) gestures, but I wasn't about to take no for an answer. Only authorized personnel are allowed to operate Emergency Exits, so I made her pull the big handle Out, then Up (as instructed by the decal).

It opened with a big "whoosh" that ripped the door right off, no surprise: it's windy out there at 500+ mph. She was still holding on, so she went with it, spinning like a top. Anybody could see everything up that short dress. Meanwhile, the kid had left his seat and was holding onto my leg as if he were trying to tackle me, for dear life, so he went with me when I dove out after her.

He was wearing an Opryland T-shirt like his "dad" and trying to bite me, so I shook him off. He could have stayed in his seat, and should have, but he didn't. We fell side by side for a minute or so (or so it seemed; it was probably less) with him reaching out for something to grab, while I unzipped my carry-on, and then he was gone.

How many guys carry a parasail in their carry-on? If that question was asked of, say, a studio audience, only one peson in the audience could raise his hand legitimately.

That would be me.

I could see the flight attendant getting smaller and smaller below as I adjusted my parasail for the optimum glide angle. The kid, too. I never saw either of them actually hit, but I figured it had to be bad. Meanwhile, it was cold and it takes a certain concentration to fly those things, even though it looks easy. It's the things that look easiest that are the hardest, often.

I descended in big circles. That way you can study the scene below and look for a good place to land. There was Kentucky Lake and Barkley Lake, side by side, and the Ohio River to the north. It felt good to see that I had been right all along, even though I had never doubted it. It was nice to know that my actions had been justified all along.

I concentrated on my glide angle, and when I looked down again there was only one lake in sight. I didn't know which one, not that it mattered; they are both just alike.

I was trying to decide whether to land on the water or

on the shore, which was all stickers it looked like, when I saw the boat.

It was barely put-putting along, a houseboat with a flat roof. I made a pretty soft landing, and almost "stuck it" except for getting my feet tangled in a plastic rope somebody had left up there. But no big deal.

I must have made a "thump" because two people came out of the cabin, onto this little deck in back, and they were staring up at me. One of them was a girl in a bikini. The other was this fat hillbilly type guy in one of those free hats they love, only this one had a gold anchor on the front, like that made him a sea captain or something. He looked pissed. I could see that this was going to be one of those days.

"Hey!" he said.

"Hey yourself," I replied, and I shot him purely as a precaution. It was the first time I had actually fired the gun. I thought I had missed, because he just sort of sat down, and I was about to shoot again, but then I saw the blood spreading all over the front of his shirt like a map, and I clicked the safety on. I had no idea how many shots were in the gun. I didn't even know what kind it was! You know how it is when you get busy, and I was still in action mode.

I took a moment to examine it. It was a Glock nine, so I figured if the clip was full (and why wouldn't it be?) there were still six or seven shots left. No point in wasting them, though. I climbed down to the rear deck on a little ladder that was there just for that purpose and almost kicked over a tackle box that was at the bottom, like a step. All the shit inside was rusty but there was a knife, of course. There is no such thing as a tackle box without a knife, in my experience.

Though how they ever cleaned fish with that one is beyond me. I had to use it like a saw to open his throat.

Then I realized that the girl was gone. How unlike me to forget a girl in a bikini! The door to the cabin was glass and I could see her inside. She was holding a shotgun in one hand and opening drawers with the other, like crazy. I figured she was looking for shells. The door was locked but I kicked it till it splintered and smashed my way in and took the shotgun away from her, and just in time—there were the shells, in the last drawer.

I scooped up five and loaded the shotgun, a Mossberg 500, and stuck the pistol in my belt. No point in waving both around. She was backed up against a little orange couch and I sat her down, with a push, just to let her know who was now in charge. Now the Captain, as it were.

Meanwhile, the houseboat was going in circles, so I took the wheel and straightened it out. I had had enough of circles descending! It was a little wooden wheel with spokes, just like a ship would have, only much smaller. An aftermarket add-on, no doubt.

The girl was just sitting there watching me. Woman, really, but I like to call them girls. She looked real cute in her bikini, and I told her so.

She didn't say anything.

"What lake are we on?" I asked, to break the ice. Plus I was curious.

Her mouth moved but she didn't say anything.

"Barkley Lake or Kentucky Lake?" I asked, to help her out.

"B-Barkley," she said.

I nodded as if I had known all along; and in a sense, I had, within a fifty percent margin of error. I knew it had to be one or the other, which was where this whole business had started.

She kept staring out the door toward the rear deck, which was a mess. I had gone a little overboard, so to speak, and the guy's head was half off. She looked kind of horrified, which was understandable, so I made her stand up and take the wheel (which would keep her looking straight ahead, or so I thought!) while I went out and "tidied up" as my mother used to say. The deck was slick with all that helpful blood and the dead guy just slid right off, under the railing and into the water.

When I came back in I was wearing the "Captain's hat," which I thought was a nice touch. The girl was still freaked out, though. Which was understandable. The guy could have been her father or her husband, either one. She was about twenty-something.

She looked real cute in her bikini and I told her so.

"D-don't," she said.

Apparently she stuttered. I pretended not to notice. When I was a kid I knew a guy in Boy Scouts who stuttered and we all pretended not to notice, to spare his feelings. I say "all"; *some* of us pretended not to notice while others were more cruel. I used to tell them, "Cruelty is not a merit badge," which it isn't.

"D-don't," she said again. She was backed up against the wheel, staring at me instead of steering.

Don't what? But I knew what she was thinking. "Don't worry," I said. "I'm a TVA baby."

That got her attention. I turned her around and showed her how to hold the wheel so the boat would go straight. I showed her from behind, being careful not to bump up against her bikini. She was finding it hard to relax.

Meanwhile, I had other problems. The gas gauge, which I could see over her strapless shoulder, was on empty! They must have been bringing the boat in when I had arrived, seemingly out of nowhere. In fact, I could see the marina, up ahead about a half a mile, tucked into a cove along the shore.

They say that when one door shuts another opens. I pointed at the marina, and she said "Aye aye, Sir." Not really, but that's what I imagined she might have said had she been more relaxed. She steered straight for it, though.

Houseboats are nothing if not slow, so I "fished" a cigarette out of my carry-on and went out onto the tiny little front deck for a smoke. I offered her one but she apparently didn't smoke. Or maybe she had been trying to quit.

High up above I could see the vapor trail of the jet, already being scattered by the stratospheric winds. Ahead, in the water, I could see something that looked like a log.

I checked it out as we putted by, at about the speed of a walk-on-the-water walk. It was the flight attendant, with her arms and legs stretched out, as if she were still falling through the air. Transitions are like that: the old persists into the new. She was face down in the water, so I figured she hadn't survived the fall, which people rarely do, so I signaled the girl to just keep us going, which she did. I was worried about the gas.

Another "log" was coming up, and this one was the little boy. The kid. "Ned." He was face up and his eyes were open so I grabbed his legs and pulled him on board, still without slowing down. I figured a lot of starting and stopping was the last thing we needed.

"Where am I?" he asked.

"Barkley Lake," I said. "It's the Cumberland River dammed up. TVA."

"Where's my dad?"

I pointed up. You could still see what was left of the vapor trail, but the plane was long gone.

"You killed him," he said.

"You don't know that for sure," I said. Actually, I had, but the last thing I needed was some hysterical kid on my hands. His clothes were all wet and his bones were all broken, so I scooped him up and put him inside on the little orange sofa. I propped him up and sat the girl down beside him. The marina was coming up and it was time for me to take the wheel.

"This is 'Ned,'" I said. I didn't know her name.

"He killed my father," the kid said. She just stared at him, horrified, then at me.

"It was his own fault," I explained back over my shoulder while I steered. "All this is top secret. Navy business. I'm a Navy Seal, and I was sent to take care of him. It's OK."

None of this was strictly true, but I have read about the Navy Seals. They are a tough bunch of customers.

"Really?" he asked.

"Shut up," I said.

That shut him up, for a while. Meanwhile, the girl was eyeing the water, like she wanted to dive in and escape, which she could have done in her bikini, so I tied her legs together with a piece of plastic rope. It was time for me to concentrate on pulling in at the marina, which I did. Very smoothly, I might add.

The gas guy came out to help us tie up. Another hillbilly, also wearing a captain's anchor hat. He saw all the blood on the rear deck and registered alarm, saying:

"What the fuck?"

"Help," said the girl, speaking up, finally.

"He killed my dad," the kid said.

They were both trying to get me in trouble. The gas guy was backing away, still registering alarm, so I killed him with the shotgun as a precaution. It made a mess of his face, and the girl started screaming. I should have aimed lower.

Luckily, there seemed to be no one else around.

I had to help her off the boat, since her legs were tied together; and I had to carry the kid, since all his bones were broken. It was turning out to be one of those days.

"Stop that damn screaming," I said, and she did. I sat her down beside the kid and instructed her to sit tight while I checked out the cars in the parking lot. I had had enough of boats, and how many guys carry a key for every kind of car in their carry-on? Pickups, too.

Again, mine would be the only hand raised.

I wanted something inconspicuous, so I settled on a Camry and put the kid and the girl in the back seat. First I made sure the gas gauge said full. On second thought, I made the girl in the bikini ride up front with me, where I could keep an eye on her.

"Fasten your seat belts," I said. "We're in for a bumpy ride." That's from a Bette Davis movie. You'll never see Bette

Davis in a bikini. And it was pretty bumpy till we got to the highway, then it smoothed out, suddenly.

"I want my mother," said the kid from the back seat.

"Then you're in luck," I said. "She's your mother now. And I'm your new dad. We're on our way to get married as soon as we find a preacher."

All white lies, of course. I'm a TVA baby, not about to marry her or anybody for that matter. But the last thing I needed was a homesick kid on my hands.

"Isn't that right, honey?" I asked.

She was no help. Her eyes were closed. We were doing about ninety. I could see the kid in the back, in the rear-view mirror. His eyes were wide open. "You killed my dad," he said.

His was a real one-note song.

"The Navy sent me," I persisted. "I'm a Blue Angel. I'm your new dad. And she's your new mom. It's all going to be OK as soon as we find us a preacher."

"It was OK before," he said. I could tell he didn't believe me.

"Just shut up," I said. I looked for something on the radio. To my surprise, they were already going on about the plane and the door and all the people falling out. Apparently there were others. I figured they must have radioed down the news and got everybody all stirred up.

Sure enough, there was a roadblock up ahead—two cop cars in a V formation, and a bunch of "smokies" with those hats and vests and the like. Luckily, I was prepared for just such an eventuality. How many guys carry blue lights in their carry-ons? I stuck mine on the dash and it confused them just long enough for me to crash through on cruise control. The smokies all jumped out of the way, all but one. The rest were shooting but they can't shoot worth a dime. I thought things would settle down once we got past, but the ones that survived insisted on following like a swarm of angry bees.

My left rear tire was thumping so I guess they weren't such bad shots after all. Apologies, etc. Luckily, there was a Wal-Mart just ahead. They carry everything.

One thing I hate about Wal-Mart is the way they are all over you as soon as you walk in, saying, "How can I help you today?" It's like they are in a hurry to get you out of there. They don't bother you, though, when you are waving a shotgun like a magic wand. Everybody sort of melted away as soon as we came in. It was almost like the place was empty, except I figured there were people ducked down here and there in the various aisles.

I dumped the kid into a shopping cart and made the girl push it. Her legs were still tied together, so she had to sort of hop. How often do you see a girl in a bikini in Wal-Mart? She looked cute and I told her so, but she just glared at me. I got some cereal and milk for later, and some bullets and a little hiking tent. It was time to give up on the car. The bullets were hollow points. "Do you know how to set up a tent?" I asked the kid.

He wasn't speaking either. Believe me, I was getting tired of these two! There was no time to waste, so I raced to the check-out area. They have several lanes but they were all empty; no check-out girls.

I wasn't about to stand on ceremony. "Looks like we get a freebie," I said.

Then I saw the check-out girl hiding under the counter, her make-up all smeared. I made her stand up and reached into my pocket for my billfold. I wanted to make things as legal as possible under the circumstances, as long as it didn't take too long, but wouldn't you know it, my billfold was missing! I figured it must have fallen out of my pocket somewhere in the descent from the commercial airliner, earlier. That's why parachutists wear special pants, with all those special pockets, I suppose.

"J-just g-go," the check-out girl said. She was also afflicted with a stutter. I was running out of patience, so I made her give me all the money out of the cash register, and gave her two twenties back.

"Keep the change," I said. It was a joke but she didn't get it. Neither did the kid.

"You can't pay her with her own money," he said. "That doesn't count."

Now he was mister logic. He was all folded up in the cart, like a rubber midget, with his eyes wide open. "Navy Seals don't steal," he said.

"Sometimes they do," I said. "I'm a Blue Angel anyway." I did my hands like wings.

"No you're not," he said. "You're a TVA baby."

He said it with a certain admiration in his eyes, so I told him the truth, which was that indeed I was. I was tired of pretending anyway. "Now you know why that 'dad' of yours had to die," I said. "He had it all wrong."

He just stared at me, all owl-eyed. I peeled off another twenty, to make it up to him. His fingers weren't broken but his arms were, so I stuck it in his wet shirt pocket. That took some doing. Meanwhile, I had forgotten the girl in the bikini. She was trying to hop away. I caught up with her, no big deal, and herded her back with the shotgun and said, "Now, let's get the hell out of here, on the double!"

Easier said than done. We started out the door but the parking lot out front was filled with police cars, all with blue lights flashing. There were Darth Vader types in black helmets crouched behind them, looking ready for action.

"Change in plans," I said.

"N-no shit, Sherlock," said the girl. She was getting saucy. I liked that. I gave her a twenty and she stuck it down the front of her bikini. I liked that too. I gave her another, then steered her and the cart toward the back of the store. It was slow going with her hopping, but I couldn't help push the cart since I had my carry-on in one hand and the shotgun in the other.

It wasn't my job to push anyway.

"Y-you're t-toast," she said. She was still stuttering, or maybe it was the hopping. I decided to ignore her. Besides, I had other things on my mind. I knew that if I could get to the loading dock I could escape into the woods out back. There's a woods behind every Wal-Mart.

Unfortunately, the loading dock was also filled with pissed-off-looking Darth Vader types.

"T-trapped!" she said. She seemed pleased. I was getting tired of her shit. "Don't be so sure," I snarled. I poked her in the butt with the shotgun and we headed for the TV section, which is, in my opinion, the nicest part of the store. All those TVs going at once, all tuned to the same station. It's almost like home.

They were all showing the "Breaking News," which was the scene out front, the parking lot crowded with cop cars with blue lights flashing. There was even a helicopter. It was Live.

"You're toast," she said again. I never liked that expression. Toast always seemed to me like something nice. I was explaining this to her and the kid while I was setting up the tent (they were no help) when she said, "I don't know why you keep talking to him. He's dead."

I stopped, taken aback.

So that was it! The open eyes had fooled me. But what about all the things he had said? Had I only imagined he was talking to me? It was entirely possible, I knew. Perhaps he had been dead all along. There was no way to know for sure. He was cold but that could have been the water. His clothes were still wet.

"So what?" I said, to give the impression that I had known all along. I made her get in the tent and topped off the pistol with the hollow points. The shotgun still had four shells.

Meanwhile, on the TV, all the Darth Vader types were coming in the front door. I turned around to look and, sure enough, I could see them toward the front of the store, darting around the aisles, trying to stay out of my line of sight.

They were moving in from the loading dock, too. Luckily, I still had a trick or two up my sleeve.

How many guys carry a universal remote in their carry-on? (Raise your hand!) I flipped around until I had Oprah on all the screens. I was waiting for her to stop talking when one screen exploded. They were shooting.

I stood up and emptied a clip and sent a bunch of shit flying, and that quieted them down again. They are kind of chicken, really. But there was a bunch of them and they were getting closer. I really needed to get out of there.

Oprah was still yakking away. I crouched down and flipped around till I got Ellen. That's more my kind of show anyway. I watch it all the time. You can't even tell she's a lesbian, not that that matters to anybody anymore.

"You," Ellen said. "What do you want?" She didn't look pleased to see me, but I'm used to that. I'm a TVA baby.

"I want to be on your show," I said.

"I told you, I don't arrange that," she said. "That's all arranged through the producer."

"It's an emergency," I said. "Can't we make an exception just this once?"

I pointed toward the front of the store, where the Darth Vader types were still filtering in, all crouched down. But of course, Ellen couldn't see *out of* the TV.

"It's not up to me," she said. "It seems to people like it is, but actually it's not."

"So what am I supposed to do?"

"Try *Wild Kingdom.*"

That was an idea. I flipped around till I found it. Two lions were eating an antelope, one from the front and one from the back.

I flipped back to Ellen. "No way," I said. I told her what I had seen and she gave a little shudder. "I can't believe that's what they call appropriate programming for children," she said.

"Meanwhile, we have a problem here," I said. "They're closing in and there's at least a hundred of them." That was an exaggeration but not by much. Down every aisle I could see crouching shapes, darting here and there.

"I have a guest," Ellen said. Sure enough, she was standing up to hug some guy in jeans and a sport coat. Some lucky dude.

"What about me?" I asked. "What am I supposed to do?"

She shrugged. "Shoot it out?"

That was no help. Oprah would have said the same. I was beginning to see that they were all cut out of the same piece of cloth. They want no surprises on their shows. I could even understand their point of view but meanwhile I had enough to worry about, with the Darth Vader types showing up down almost every aisle.

I fired off another clip, my last.

"You're trapped," said the girl in the bikini. She was peering out the window of the tent. I made her zip it shut from inside and told her to shut her pie hole while I went to the guns & ammo section. I had to crawl. I had to break the glass. I was reloading with hollow points when I heard a voice over the store's PA system:

"Drop the gun and come out with your hands on your head!"

It's usually used to announce sales and such. I guess they figured it made them sound more official, and to be perfectly honest, it did. It gave me a shiver.

I was getting worried.

I crawled back to the TV section. A guy tried to stop me on the way but he was too slow, and I wasted him with one shot. The hollow points expand. Somebody pulled him out of the way, sliding him back in his own helpful blood. The dudes were everywhere.

I had a sinking feeling when I saw the tent, and when I picked up one side to look underneath, sure enough, the girl was gone, bikini and all. She had somehow split the scene.

Now there was just me and the kid, who was still in the shopping cart, and dead besides. "Ned" was no help. Another TV exploded but there were still plenty left.

I tried Ellen again. "What about the studio audience?" I suggested.

She ignored me, as was often her wont. Meanwhile, bullets were flying all around. Not one to stand on ceremony, I squeezed on through, and just in time. Bullets were smacking into my flesh.

The chairs for the studio audience were arranged in rows, on low risers. None had arms. Everybody was watching Ellen, who was holding a puppy on her lap.

"Scoot," I said, but all I got were blank looks. Scoot, it turns out, was the name of the puppy.

"Scoot over!" I said in a loud whisper, to which I added a snarl, and over they scooted, all of them at once.

And just in time for the commercial break. The lights went weird. I took my seat just in time as Ellen looked up from her puppy and asked, pretending to be interested (they are always pretending), "And how many TVA babies do we have in our studio audience today?"

Mine was, as always, as ever, the only hand raised.

Private Eye

"**S**pare one of those?"

"Of course." I shook a Camel out of my pack, which was sitting on the bar as a reminder of better days. She was wearing a raincoat—Burberry; we notice such things—over jeans. It matched her hair, almost; it wasn't buttoned, only belted at the waist. She was three stools away, but I caught a glimpse of a narrow black strap on a narrow pale shoulder when she leaned down the bar to take the cigarette from my fingers.

We notice such things. Especially in a quiet bar on Eighth Avenue, on a rainy Thursday autumn-in-New York afternoon.

She was careful not to touch my fingers; I was careful not to touch hers. I have a lot of respect for cigarettes, these days.

"Thanks."

Her hair was what they used to call dirty blonde, cut short. Full, red lips and a low, smoky voice with eyes to match: dark, deep Jeanne Moreau eyes, filled with a certain sorrowful something. Regret? Loss? Perhaps. She was coasting, like me, on the high side of forty and her face looked it, which I found appealing, and her body didn't, which we find appealing. So many young girls have empty eyes.

"You're welcome," I said.

She sat back and examined the cigarette as if it were a fish she'd caught. Holding both ends in long fingers, very deft. Great hands. A dancer's hands.

Then she lit it!

She tapped it on the bar and put it between her lips and struck a match and lit it.

Inhaled.

Exhaled.

I turned on my stool, alarmed, but the bartender was paying no attention. The little faux bistro—there's one on every block in the west twenties—was empty except for us.

"Excuse me," I said, sliding my drink down the bar and taking a seat next to hers. "But I thought you couldn't smoke in New York bars anymore."

"You can't," she said. "But Lou cuts me a pass every afternoon at about this time, when the lunch crowd's gone."

It was ten after two.

"Extraordinary," I said, tapping a Camel out of my pack. "Perhaps if I pretended to be with you, Lou would cut me a pass, too?"

"Depends." She eyed me sideways. "Are you a good pretender?"

"Good?" I contrived to sound like I was trying to sound insulted. "I'm the Great Pretender. Plus you'll probably want another anyway." I laid the pack down like a high card. Maybe even a trump, I was thinking.

"As long as we are pretending," she said. "Just don't get any ideas."

"Ideas?" My head was filled with ideas. "I never get ideas."

"I'm here to take a break," she said. "Not to get hit on. As long as you understand that, we can pretend we are friends. I'll even pretend to enjoy your company."

Not to mention my Camels.

"Not to mention your Camels," she added.

Lou did, indeed, cut me a pass. And she did enjoy my company, or at least pretend. And I hers. She was an "Internet worker bee" (or so she called it, then) who worked at home, right around the corner. I was, well, whatever I told her I was.

"Burberry," I said. "An old boyfriend?"

"All my boyfriends are old," she said. "The young are too needy."

"So many young girls have empty eyes," I said, and ordered us both a wine. White for her, red for me.

Her coat fell open when she leaned forward to pick up her glass. I saw the top of a slip, black silk, or something very like it. The strap was loose which told me that her breasts were probably small. But we couldn't see enough to tell.

"What is it with you guys and straps?" she asked, lighting another Camel off the one she was smoking. "It's not like you're actually *seeing* anything."

Busted. Even honesty is, sometimes, the best policy. "Extrapolation," I said.

"Beg your pardon?"

"Each part suggests the whole. That inch and a half of narrow strap, seen as if by accident, suggests the lacy cup to which it leads, which in turn suggests that which it cups, shapes, presents. That little strap takes the mind's eye to where the eye alone can't, quite, yet, go. Extrapolation."

"Well said," she said. I thought so too. She blew an

almost-perfect smoke ring, then looked me straight in the eye and asked: "How many of you are there?"

Busted again. I glanced at my Fauxlex. "Sixty-seven, as of now. They come and go. How'd you know?"

"I read about it in *Wired*," she said. "Cyberhosting. Private Eyes. It's the new new thing. And a girl can tell. There's a certain—intensity of regard."

"Well said," I said. "And you don't mind?"

"On the contrary, it's kind of appealing." She leaned forward and the Burberry fell open, just enough. "Especially since *regard* is all that's involved."

"There are Protocols," I said. There was that lovely intimate little strap again. "Appropriate for just such an occasion."

"Well said," she said, sliding off her stool. "It's almost three. Tell you what: you may come up till five."

She picked up my Camels and left the bar. Scarcely believing our luck, I touched my Fauxlex to the bill strip, beeped Lou a fifty to cover the tip, and followed.

☆   ☆   ☆

Her name, she told me in the elevator, was Eula. I didn't realize, then, what it meant. Her place was a mess. It was a studio filled with computers, monitors, cables, drives, all the apparatus with which I am, ironically, so unfamiliar. One high window (dirty), one houseplant (dying), one futon couch facing a cluttered coffee table on a faded fake Persian rug.

With a nod, she sat me down on the rug. Then she slipped off her Burberry, hung it carefully on the back of a chair stacked with computer manuals, and disappeared into her tiny kitchen. She came back with two white-wine glasses and a bottle to match. Pinot Grigio.

She sat on the couch with her long legs tucked underneath her. "So you are cyberhosting," she said. "There was an article in *Playboy* too. What's it like, being a Private Eye? Been at it long?"

The strap, both straps, led down to a black slip with lacy cups tucked into tight, faded jeans. High-end tank top.

"A few months," I said. "Nobody's been doing it long. It's a new technology, the nanobiotech thing. My clients log in and they see what I see."

She lit a Camel and tossed me my pack. "And that's it?"

"Private Eyes operate under very strict Protocols," I said. "No physical contact. My clients would be bounced off immediately, were I to touch even your fingertips. And I would be out of a job."

I had been wrong about her breasts. No bra, as far as we could tell. And we could almost tell.

"And that suits them—your clients?"

"It seems to. My clients are all lookers. See-onlys. Perhaps they have been disappointed in love. Perhaps a look is all they want."

"And yourself?" She shrugged one strap off one narrow shoulder. That made both shoulders, somehow, even more appealing.

"I'm kind of a looker myself."

"So I see." She blew a smoke ring. "But isn't it weird?"

"Being a looker?"

"Having all those strangers lurking inside you."

"They're not actually inside me," I said. "It's virtual. A Private Eye is just a sender, that's all."

"They watch on a screen?"

"You must not have read the whole article; they just close their eyes. It's all bio, like I said. They suck on a chip and close their eyes and see what I see. Satellite link."

"A chip. Like hard candy. What if they swallow it?"

"They don't. All the sensories are in the mouth. You don't taste with your stomach, do you? Besides it's rather expensive."

"I like that part," she said. "And where do you find them? These clients?"

"I don't have to. I have no idea who they are. They buy the chip and surf all the different Private Eyes."

"So it's a kind of competition."

"I suppose. I do OK. All I have to do is find a pretty girl to talk to."

"Or woman," she said. "And peep down her dress."

"Or her Burberry."

"And get paid for it."

"A modest sum," I said. "As long as I observe the Protocols. Plus I get expenses."

"The cigarettes." She kicked off her shoes, or rather slippers; or rather, pulled them off by the heels with long dancer's toes, one and then the other.

"I pay for the Camels," I said. "The bar tab goes through my Fauxlex. I only host on weekday afternoons, one to six."

"Free drinks," she said. She crossed her legs. Her jeans were pulled tight, making a wide V between her thighs. "And can they hear all this?"

"They're see-onlys," I said. "No sound, according to Private Eye."

"So they miss out on all the conversation?"

"They don't seem to mind."

"Am I suppose to be flattered?" she asked.

The apartment darkened as the afternoon light dimmed. We talked of mystery novels and Tenth Avenue bars, until she looked at her watch and sent me away.

"It's five," she said at the door.

"What does that have to do with anything?" I was surprised to find I hadn't been pretending to enjoy her company.

"Protocols," she said, and shut the door.

"You're back," she said the next afternoon. Friday.

"By popular demand," I said, laying my Camels on the bar. I showed her the counter on my Fauxlex.

"Seventy. Your numbers are up. I suppose I should be flattered again."

"I suppose. I would be."

We bothered Lou just twice, once for wine and once for matches, before she headed upstairs and I followed, exactly at three.

"Don't you have a girlfriend?" she asked, in the elevator.

"I did and then I didn't," I said, following her into her studio. "You know how it goes."

"I do." She slipped off the Burberry and hung it on the chair before sitting down on the couch, across the low table from me.

"I find this more intimate anyway," I said. "Being a Private Eye."

"Not so very private," she reminded me. Instead of jeans over the slip, she wore black tights under it.

"And you don't mind?"

"On the contrary," she said. She stretched out one long dancer's leg and pulled the other up under her chin. "So where's your chip? Stick out your tongue and let me see."

"It's not a chip, it's a nanocoil." I tapped one eyebrow. "Wrapped around an optic dendrite. A painless laser insert, on a timer, like I said."

"Cool," she said. "And this three score and ten from one to six, do you feel them looking through your eyes?"

"I'm not supposed to, but there's a little feedback. When they see something they like, there is a kind of glow."

"So you can tell when they are pleased." She spread her thighs, a little.

"Sometimes. Like right now. They can see the pale outline of your panties through your tights, like a ghost, hiding in the shadows."

She held up two fingers and I lit a Camel for her.

"And they like ghosts," I added.

"And you?"

"I like ghosts. And shadows, too." I leaned across the coffee table, and she took the cigarette between her fingers, being careful not to touch mine. It was an oddly intimate move.

"I see," she said. She stretched out her long legs and there was that ghost again. "And if those fingers had touched?"

"My coil would shut down. They would all go find another Private Eye."

"And you would be out of a job."

"It's only a part-time job," I said.

We do like ghosts. The afternoon light faded as we talked of de Kooning and Long Island wine, and cities we both knew, and some that we didn't.

Until exactly five, when she saw me out. In the elevator, and later, on the street, I felt my clients, like a flock of birds, departing into an autumn dusk.

I felt the glow fading.

I was sorry it was Friday.

It's only a part-time job, but I love it.

I miss it on weekends, when I'm off. Sometimes—OK, most of the time—I ramble around the Web, looking for the kind of women I look for when I'm working; the kind who like to be looked at.

Regarded with a certain intensity.

Still, I was surprised when I found her on the Web.

Eula-Cam. Live. Updated Daily, for Members Only.

I scrolled through the Free Stills, and there she was, sitting on the couch in her black slip over black tights, ghostly, talking to a guy on the rug.

His back was to the camera but I knew who it was.

Me.

"You might have told me," I said on Monday, laying my Camels on the bar.

"What?"

"That we're in the same business." I raised two fingers and Lou brought two wines, one white, one red. "You're a jenni. A cam girl."

"Busted," she said. She was wearing the Burberry over the straps. But the jeans were gone, and the tights too. "You're a smart guy. I figured you would figure it out for yourself."

I considered that while we sipped and smoked. The bare legs were intriguing.

"I suppose I should be flattered," I said.

"I would be. Besides, we're not exactly in the same business, you know."

"We're not?"

"Your clients are looking *through* you. My clients are looking *at* me."

"So are mine," I said. "Which makes you the principal attraction. The main event. The feature presentation."

"Well said," she said. "Got a problem with that?"

I didn't have a problem with that.

"Me neither." She picked up my cigarettes and left. I beeped the bill strip and followed.

She slipped out of the Burberry and hung it over the chair, carefully. I was looking over my shoulder.

"Looking for the cam? It's built into the TV," she said.

I saw it: a little green light, like an eye. There was a number underneath it: 04436.

"Those are your numbers? I'm impressed." I said.

"But not surprised. It's on all the time?"

"It's green when it's on and it's on when I'm here. And I have to be here except between one and three, when I'm on break."

"MicroCam pays the rent?"

"That would be slavery," she said. She contrived to look insulted. "Or worse. I'm just paying off a debt."

She pointed at the computer in the corner. Even I had heard of the XLinteL99. It purred silently like an expensive cat.

"All I have to do is be myself. And, of course, observe the Protocols."

"And what are your Protocols?"

"Quite strict. The Internet's not free anymore, you know. I'm on a soft-user open-public band. No nipples, no pubic hair; no nudity except when I'm alone."

"Alone with your four thousand guys," I reminded her, nodding toward the TV.

"And no visitors, except between three and five."

"I suppose I should be flattered," I said. And was.

"I suppose you should." She sat down on the couch across from me. As she crossed her legs I caught a glimpse of white panties. Not the ghost but the real thing.

"Sorry to disappoint," she said.

"Do I look disappointed?"

She pointed at my wrist. "Your numbers are down."

I checked my Fauxlex. Fifty-five. Then fifty-four.

"That's them, not me. They come and go. Maybe they don't like your Protocols."

"I thought you said they couldn't hear us."

"Maybe they can read lips," I said. Hers were deep red.

"Hope you don't get paid by the client."

I did but I didn't mind. She stretched out one leg and showed me her panties again. Narrow, silk, edged with lace. "It's more intimate, this way," I said. "Just us forty-two. And your four thousand."

"Five." She pointed at the TV: 05035. "You must be good for business." She leaned forward to set down her wine, holding the top of her slip closed with long fingers, like a card player hiding her hand. It was only barely effective.

I felt a glow. I told her so.

"Even with your numbers down?"

"It must be my own."

We talked of movies and restaurants. We shared many favorites. It was not surprising. We were colleagues, in a way, after all.

At precisely five she saw me out. "Protocols."

I felt my clients departing, all thirty-four of them.

She was killing my business, but I didn't care.

I hurried home.

Eula-Cam.

I scrolled through her Free Stills. There she was, carefully taking a cigarette from my fingers without touching them. Even though cams have no sound, I could hear her voice in my head. Low, smoky, intimate—

I clicked on the next Free Still.

She had just closed the door after seeing me out. I clicked again and she was starting to pull her slip off over her head. I happened to know she wasn't wearing a bra.

Or was it wearing no bra?

I clicked again, a little too eagerly, and a new screen came up: End User Licensing Agreement.

EULA.

I scrolled through it. All I wanted was to see her nipples. All it wanted was my credit card number, and my scout's honor that I was Over 18.

I almost clicked on *I Agree*.

Almost. Then I thought of the five thousand other guys and went to the movie instead. I saw Meg Ryan's nipples along with a hundred other guys.

I went to bed feeling lonely for the first time in months.

On Tuesday Lou brought two wines without asking, white and red. I tapped out two Camels.

"Eula," I said. "End User Licensing Agreement. I'm a little slow but I got it. What's your real name?"

"I'm not allowed to say," she said. "Protocols."

"Am I allowed to extrapolate?"

"Isn't that your specialty?" She leaned forward to get a light. The Burberry fell open and there was that dear little strap. But tight, not loose, and pink, not black. "But why extrapolate when you can see everything on the Web?"

"With five thousand other guys?" I lit her Camel for her. "I prefer the intimacy of a private conversation."

"Even when it ruins your business?" She pointed at my Fauxlex. It was down to twenty-one.

"It's not a business," I said. "It's a part-time job."

"I suppose I should be flattered," she said, picking up my cigarettes.

It was 2:55. "I suppose you should," I said. I beeped the bill strip and followed.

☆   ☆   ☆

I sat down on the rug and watched while she spread her Burberry carefully over the back of its chair.

She wore a black half-slip and a little pink brassiere. Cups edged with lace.

I checked the TV. The green light was on and the counter under it read 06564.

"So why are they here?" I asked.

"Who?"

"Your clients. Why are they even logged on when I am here? A visitor. They must know your Protocols."

"You seem to resent them," she said.

"The Protocols?"

"The clients."

I did but said I didn't. She was working, after all, just like me.

"Maybe they're romantics," she said. "It must be the suspense. Protocols are all about suspense."

"So are bras," I said. Her pink cups were not so little after all.

"Extrapolating again?" She sat on the couch, pulling the slip down between her thighs. "What is it with you guys and bras, anyway?"

"The brassiere," I said, pouring us both a glass of Pinot Grigio, "is the most romantic invention of western civilization."

"Next to the Web."

"Better. The brassiere is itself a kind of web. It traps guys. It's a kind of Protocol. It restricts, restrains. It shapes and displays that which it conceals. It focuses the regard. It presents."

"Well said," she said, adjusting her cups, first one and then the other. "Plus it keeps the green light on."

We both looked at the TV. 07865.

"Were it to come off," she said, "the light would go red and they would all be gone." She reached out for a cigarette.

"I wouldn't miss them," I said. I gave her one and lit it, being careful not to touch her fingers with my own.

"I might," she said. "They're paying for my XLinteL99."

We talked of sports and sonnets and she saw me out at five.

I felt my clients departing, all eighteen of them. I still could feel the glow.

Eula-Cam.

I scrolled through her Free Stills until I was gone. She was on the couch, alone, in bra and panties, putting on lipstick. The label said Deep Rose.

I clicked. She was reaching behind her back with long fingers to unhook her bra.

I clicked again and I was at the end of the Free Stills. END USER LICENSE AGREEMENT.

I almost clicked on I AGREE. Then I thought of the seven thousand other guys. She was taking it off for them.

I was beginning to hate them, every one.

☆ ☆ ☆

The next day she was late, for the first time. "Where you been?"

"A girl likes to shop," she said.

"On the house," said Lou, setting down two glasses, one white, one red.

"Down to seven," she said, checking out my Fauxlex as I lit her Camel. "They're jumping ship. And yet, you're back."

"They're a fickle bunch," I said. "They like excitement. Nudity. Nipples at least."

"And you don't?"

"I'm a romantic, remember? Intimacy's my thing."

"Hard candy's mine," she said, puckering her lips. "That's what I was shopping for."

I followed her upstairs. She folded her Burberry over the chair and let me watch her walk across the room in bra and panties. It was a different bra. I could see her nipples through it.

Round little shadows. "Doesn't count," she said, looking down approvingly. "As long as they're covered."

"Protocols," I said. Her panties were sheer too, except for the little triangle that barely covered her pubic hair. Even with just eight clients—no, nine—I was glowing like a stove.

"Now they're back," she said, leaning over me to glance at my Fauxlex. "What is it with you guys and panties, anyway?" She sat down on the couch with her feet pulled up underneath her and her knees just slightly apart.

"Honey, do you have to ask?" I thought that was clever.

Instead of answering, she closed her eyes and leaned way back.

"It's the little triangle," I said. White silk, or something very like it, pulled tight between her thighs. "It's like the pubic hair I'm not allowed to see. It says, *Here*."

"Well said," she said, lifting one leg and hugging her knee to her breast. The triangle narrowed to a soft white lane that led down out of sight. The silk road.

Her eyes were closed. Mine were wide. I felt a glow.

"They present. Like the brassiere, they display what they conceal," I said. "There's a certain intimacy in the presentation."

"And in the regard as well," she said, her eyes still closed.

I supposed I should be flattered.

"Indeed, you should," she said. She opened her eyes and reached out for a Camel, carefully, and we shared the wine and talked of cabbages and kings.

The silk road faded in the failing light.

At five she showed me out, and I felt my clients fleeing. All but one. He stayed with me till six, and so did the glow.

Eula Cam.

I clicked through Free Stills, and there she was in bra and panties, seeing me out. Closing the door with the fingertips I had never touched.

I could almost hear her saying, "Tomorrow, then?"

Tomorrow, then.

I clicked again and those same fingertips were inside the waistband of her panties, about to slip them down.

I clicked again and the EULA filled the screen.

I wasn't even tempted to click on *I Agree*. It wasn't what I wanted.

I clicked BACK until I found her putting on her lipstick. Deep Rose.

I left it there. What I wanted was to read her lips with mine.

☆   ☆   ☆

"What's with the hard candy," I said. "Are you trying to quit smoking?"

"Hardly." She reached for my Camels, tapping the pack on the bar. "A girl likes to have something to suck."

"Sorry, guys," said Lou. "I got a complaint. You'll have to take the cigarettes outside."

"We have to talk," I said, outside. "I'm thinking of quitting my job."

"I've been thinking too," she said, in the elevator, looking up at me. I leaned over to kiss her but she stepped back, just one step.

The elevator door opened.

"Don't do anything rash," she said, glancing at my Fauxlex. "You still have one client left."

I was feeling rash. "I'm feeling rash," I said.

"It's a sort of new feeling, isn't it," she said, hanging the Burberry carefully over its chair. "For such as us."

I nodded. She was wearing little pink panties, and the not-so-little pink bra. The original again. I sat down on the rug and checked the TV.

9865.

"You could make them go away," I said.

"Too soon," she said. She pointed at the TV: 9904. "My XLinteL99 is not quite paid for."

"I can help," I said. "How much do you owe?"

"You're already helping," she said, sitting down on the couch across from me. She opened her thighs to show me her little silk road.

"I want to be alone with you," I said. "Is that too much to ask?"

"What about your cyberhosting job? You still have one client left."

"I know how get rid of him," I said. I reached for her hand but she pulled it back. Teasing me?

"Not so fast," she said. "Look."

We both looked. 10007.

"Now we can talk alone."

She reached behind her back to unhook her bra, the most intimate of moves. It would be ungentlemanly to say just what she showed me; and more ungentlemanly still to deny the glow they gave me.

The light on the TV was green at 10011, 10012, then suddenly red. 00000.

"Alone at last," she said. "My XLinteL99 is finally paid off. Now, what was it you wanted to talk about?"

"Read my lips," I said, getting up from the rug. "I still have one client to get rid of. And I know how to do it."

I reached for her hand but she pulled it back. "Not so fast," she said. "I have something to show your last client. A little farewell gift. I want you to feel the glow."

She slipped her fingertips under the waistband of her panties, just like in the still, and pulled them off. She lay back on the couch with her eyes closed. "You always said you were sort of a looker."

I sat back down. Her very white thighs were opened, very wide.

"You're something of a looker too," I said. It was only one client, but the glow was strong.

"I suppose I am," she said. She reached out to take my hand and the glow was gone as my last client was bounced. Replaced by a stronger, more intimate glow.

"I like this glow better," I said, and I kissed her.

And she kissed me. Our tongues played chase in her mouth and then in mine, and then—

"What's this?" I said. Mumbled.

She spit it out, delicately, into her hand.

It was a chip. Why was I not surprised?

"Double the pleasure," she said, tossing it onto the rug. "And double the fun. Now come here."

I came there.

☆   ☆   ☆

Five o'clock came and went. She put on her lipstick, a touch-up, and that was all. Deep Rose.

"It's Rose," I said. "Your name. I finally got it."

"I was beginning to wonder," she said, pulling on her panties and lighting a Camel, our last one. It was also white. She left off the little pink brassiere.

Her not so little nipples were also pink. Wet pink now.

"I guess we're both out of a job," she said. "What now?"

"You mean forever, or this evening?" I asked. I took the cigarette from her fingers, being careful to touch them as I did.

"Both," she said. "Let's start with this evening."

"For that, my sweet Rose," I said, "there are Protocols."

For once she looked worried. "Protocols?"

"Chinese or Thai?" I said. "Eat out or order in?"

"Thai," she said, smiling. "And I'd hate to have to dress for dinner."

"<u>I Agree</u>," I said, picking up the phone.

Pirates of the Somali Coast

From: yohoho@africanprincess.com
Subject: CRUISE
Date: July 20, 2007 9:54 AM ADT
To: mom4@aol.com

Hi Mom

Yo ho ho from your son on the High Sea at last. Aunt Bea says HLO. The cabin is so small but thats OK because the ship is so big. There aren't many other kids aboard, mostly old folks like Unc and Aunt Bea. The ship doesn't have any masts or sails but there are 2 swimming pools, one on deck and one inside that's not so nice. The sailors don't dress like sailers. They dress like waiters in a restraunt. Hope we see Pirates or have a big storm soon.

PS, thanks for the Pirate hat, Unc says it makes me look fearfull.

From: yohoho@africanprincess.com
Subject: FRIGATE
Date: July 20, 2007 10:14 AM ADT
To: bugdude@yahoo.com

Yo Bug

Yo ho ho, its me, ahoy from the High Sea. I am sailing on the frigate African Princess. Its not really a frigate but a cruise ship filled with old people, but they have a Game

Room where I can send email. Its send-only tho so I cant get any back. Mom and dad sent me on a cruise with my uncle and aunt (ugh). Well be gone a week. The games here suck but they have a kids version of Grand Theft Auto (duh). Maybe there will be sharks and Pirates. Or Rogue Waves like on that TV special.

From: yohoho@africanprincess.com
Subject: CRUISE
Date: July 21, 2007 9:06 AM ADT
To: mom4@aol.com
HI MOM

Aunt Bea says HLO. She wont go out much because she is sea sick almost every day even if the water is smooth. I am hoping for a Rogue Wave but so far everything is smooth. I saw a dolphin yesterday. They swim along the bow of the ship like they are racing it. That's the front. Tell dad HLO. Unc is in the Casino all day. He doesnt like the ocean much. He told me to muse my self so I am in the Game Room where there are 6 computers. The food is xcelent and we can have all the desert we want. There are 2 pools.

From: yohoho@africanprincess.com
Subject: KNOTS
Date: July 21, 2007 10:34 AM ADT
To: bugdude@yahoo.com
Yo Bugg

The ship is 22 thousand tons. I have a friend in the crew,

his name is Curtis and hes from Cape Town like us. Hes Coloured but very cool. He has heard of Rogue Waves but never seen one. Hes not xactly an Old Salt! Yesterday we made 194 knots which is more than 200 miles. I wish the African Princess had sails instead of big engines you cant even see. We saw a sail yesterday but it was just a yacht from Durban with a topless girl. Ugh. No Pirates yet! We are heading up the coast and will go through Suez next week. Curtis says its like driving through the desert. Maybe I will see a camel like the one we saw pissing on the school trip last year. And Arabs too! Its a canal.

From: yohoho@africanprincess.com
Subject: CRUISE NEWS
Date: July 23, 2007 5:06 PM ADT
To: mom4@aol.com

Hi Mom

There is lots to do for kids but not many kids, only 6. Two of the boys are super stupid but one has a Gameboy. There is a movie theater xpecialy for us. Today they showed Pirates of the Caribbean with Johnny Depp. I sat next to a girl named Estelle from Johannesburg. She calls it Joeburg. I never herd that before. Curtis my sailer friend, says there arent Pirates anymore and he's glad but I am not. I am wearing the Pirate hat you gave me everyday. Curtis and the crew dress like people in restraunts. Unc says HLO. He is in the Casino all day and Aunt Bea is sea sick in the cabin so it smells super bad. They dont have any friends. wish you and Dad were here.

From:　yohoho@africanprincess.com
Subject:　JOHNNY DEPP NOT
Date:　July 24, 2007 10:34 AM ADT
To:　bugdude@yahoo.com
Yo Bugg

Saw a Pirate yesterday! NOT. It was just a crew sailer named
Curtis in a Johnny Depp mask. They had a Pirate Day for
the kids and they gave us all Pirate hats but theres were just
paper. Mine was the only real one. Curtis made us all walk
the plank at the pool. His cutlass was plastic. The girls wore
there bathing suits (ugh). Then we had songs and Estelle
tried to kiss me. She is crazy. Tomorrow we are crossing
the Equator. It is an invisible line. Whats so hot about that? I
wish there were real Pirates. The ocean is BO RING! ☹

From:　yohoho@africanprincess.com
Subject:　CRUISE
Date:　July 25, 2007 5:06 PM ADT
To:　mom4@aol.com
Hi Mom

Unc lost a thousand Rand in the casino and said not to
tell Aunt Bea, like I would. Aunt Bea is still sea sick even
tho there are no waves at all. The sea is like a big pond. I
wish we had a Rogue Wave. The cabin smells like vomit.
Im sorry but it does. She says the whiskey helps but you
wouldnt think so. It's the same kind you took from her at
Christmas, Cutty Sark. That was a clipper ship. This is not
a real ship. There was an equator ceremony today and the
captain was King Neptune. He is fat! I miss you and dad to.

From: yohoho@africanprincess.com
Subject: PIRATE DAY
Date: July 26, 2007 10:34 AM ADT
To: bugdude@yahoo.com

Yo Bug

Yohoho, guess what, today was Real Pirate day! They were in a speedboat without any sails. They raced along side the Princess and shot at us with machine guns. It was cool. They were standing up in the speedboat and firing like crazy. They hit one old man and took off the side of his head, just like in the Viking Raid game only that was an ax. The captain made the ship zig zag. We have no cannons or cutlasses whatso ever. They made all the kids hide in the Game Room. That's where we are now. Estelle and I tried to sneak out to see the Pirates but they made us go back. She's not so bad. We can hear the shooting tho.

From: yohoho@africanprincess.com
Subject: PIRATE DAY
Date: July 26, 2007 4:19 PM ADT
To: bugdude@yahoo.com

Yo Dude

The Pirates were all gone when they let us out. The old people are all crying even tho only one is dead. They all ready cleaned up all the blood. Estelle looked under the sheet and saw his half head. She likes Pirate stuff. Old people donlt like Pirates or adventure at all. Whats the point of a cruise then? More later

From: yohoho@africanprincess.com
Subject: PIRATE DAY
Date: July 27, 2007 10:19 AM ADT
To: mom4@aol.com
Hi Mom

Guess what, there were Pirates yesterday, but we got away
with zig zags. I wanted to see them but the crew made
us stay in the Game Room. One old man was killed. I
have one friend, her name is Estelle. She's the one from
Joeburg. Aunt Bea wants to go home. Not me, tho. Things
are Looking Up as Dad likes to say. Curtis says maybe
more Pirates today. I have my fingers crossed. He is my
Coloured sailer friend. You would like him. He doesnt say
there arent any Pirates any more. Yo ho ho!

From: yohoho@africanprincess.com
Subject: PIRATE DAY
Date: July 27, 2007 10:19 AM ADT
To: bugdude@yahoo.com

Yo Bug

Big news! We have been captured by Pirates for real. Im not
kidding. They are the same ones in the speedboat, but this
time they had a little cannon. It was cool. They blew out all
the windows out of the Bridge with one shot. That's where
the captain mans the wheel. Talk about glass every where.
Then they boarded the ship, climbing up ropes just like in
the movies. Nobody fought them. At first I thought they were
fake because they all wore Johnny Depp masks but that was
just to scare people. They are real Pirates, about twenty, all

Arabs. They wear scarfs instead of Pirate hats, but they all have guns. Some are machine guns. Can you believe my luck? They are making all the kids stay in the Game Room. But we can hear them all ready Plundering outside.

From: yohoho@africanprincess.com
Subject: PIRATE DAY
Date: July 28, 2007 10:19 AM ADT
To: mom4@aol.com

Hi Mom

Its official. The African Princess has been captured by Pirates, and it's very xciteing. They are real Pirates. They boarded us yesterday with ropes. At first they wore Johnny Depp masks but they were just plastic so they they took them off and locked all the men in the Casino. Most of them were there already anyway. They dont have any cutlass's but they have machine guns and revolvers, plus lots of cool knives and a chainsaw to. I guess Aunt Bea is still in the cabin. I have to stay in the Game Room with the other kids. It smells better here!

From: yohoho@africanprincess.com
Subject: PIRATE WEEK
Date: July 28, 2007 3:14 PM ADT
To: bugdude@aol.com

Yo Bug

Guess what, I met the Pirate captain. His name is Ali and he is just like Jack Sparrow, for real! I told him about Pirate

Day and he said its Pirate Week now. Cool! He is the almost only one that knows English. Ali let me help with the Pillaging. He likes my hat. They lined up all the ladies and took their rings and jewels. Sometimes they just cut their fingers right off. I helped pick them up like little wurms. They were all begging for mercy, not the Pirates of course, they were laughing. Then they raped some. Ugh. That was like sex fighting. Pirates like the fat ones best. Theres lots of blood, xspecially on the stairs and they dont clean it up. It makes it more realistic. Yo ho ho

From: yohoho@africanprincess.com
Subject: PIRATE WEEK
Date: July 29, 2007 10:19 AM ADT
To: mom4@aol.com

Hi Mom

Hello from the pirate ship African Princess. I told Ali they should change the name but they are all Arabs. They are Plundering and Pillaging all the grown ups. They call them Jew Pigs. Today they poured out all the whiskey, you would like that! Two of the men were drunk so they cut there throats Pirate style. Ali says its Pirate Week! He's my favorite. Aunt Bea is hiding in the cabin tho. Still sea sick I guess, plus she doesn't like Pirate stuff.

From: yohoho@africanprincess.com
Subject: PIRATE DAY
Date: July 29, 2007 1:21 PM ADT
To: bugdude@yahoo.com

Yo Bug

The Pirates are sailing the ship now. some of the crew has joined them. Curtis who was my friend, didnt want to so they cut off his nose and threw him over board. I tried to tell him! I still have his nose. It's a souvenir of Pirate Week.

Its fun to look over the rail, there are sharks everywhere. They seem very happy with there big grins (joke). Estelle and I tried to count them but we gave up at 100. She likes Pirates to. The other kids are hope less. More later. Yr pal ☺.

From: yohoho@africanprincess.com
Subject: PIRATE DAY
Date: July 30, 2007 10:06 AM ADT
To: mom4@aol.com
Hi Mom

The trip through Suez has been called off, according to the Pirates. I guess well be heading home soon. The head Pirate is called Ali. He has lots of real tattoos. The other pirates have to do like he says. He wears a scarf around his head and even has gold teeth and a little beard. I call him Jack Sparrow and he laughs and called me matey. He's the only Pirate that speaks English and its None Too Good as Dad would say. I think he likes my Pirate hat. I have a cutlass but its plastic. I wish I had a real one.

From: yohoho@africanprincess.com
Subject: PIRATE LORE

Date: July 30, 2007 2:10 PM ADT
To: bugdude@yahoo.com

Yo Bugg

Pirates like to hang people. There are no yardarms on the African Princess so they hang them from the railings. Most of them are pretty fat so they dont kick long. The kicking is the best part. They also pee in there pants (ugh). Ali lets me tie all the knots. Can you believe Pirates don't know any knots?! I just do a bowline and a loop. I know that from Scouts and it looks noosey. You just add some xtra turns. Ali calls me Matey. He gave me a Pirate necklace made out of fingers. They are all curled up. Creepy!! I have another Pirate friend named Claude. Wish you were here. PS The worse thing about hanging is to pee in your pants!

From: yohoho@africanprincess.com
Subject: PIRATE WEEK
Date: August 1, 2007 5:12 PM ADT
To: mom4@aol.com

Hi Mom

Today we crossed the Equator again. Its an invisible line. One Pirate who is very cruel, his name is Claude was dressed up like Neptune the King of the Sea. He used the chain saw to push people in to the pool. Ali made them all line up. The Pirates were all having fun. It was the nice pool, the other ones not as nice, but now the water is pink with stuff floating in it (ugh) and Estelle is mad because she says they ruined the pool. She is a good diver. Love—

From: yohoho@africanprincess.com
Subject: PIRATE DAY
Date: August 2, 2007 10:19 AM ADT
To: bugdude@yahool.com

Yo Bug

Everyday the Pirates kill people in funny ways. Some times
they use the chain saw but its not traditional. Best of all
was when they killed the captain. Hes this fat old dude in
his underwear. They put a rat in his mouth and taped it
shut with duck tape, then we got to watch the rat eat his
face from inside. It took awhile but it was cool. Estelle got
sick. They are Plundering like crazy. One old lady hid her
gold in her bosom so they set her on fire. She was hard to
light so they used gasoline. They poured it out of the chain
saw over her big hair do. They borrowed a lighter from her
husband. She was spinning around and knocking stuff over,
so they pushed her overboard with sticks because she was
to hot to touch. She made a hissing sound like fireworks
when she hit the water. You know, the one they call the
Snake. I hollered Yo Ho Ho and Ali just laughed. Did I
tell you about Claude? He let me wear his Johnny Depp
mask. He was in the French Foreign Legion and he speaks
English to. I like him better than the Arabs Xcept for Ali.

From: yohoho@africanprincess.com
Subject: PIRATE WEEK
Date: August 2, 2007 4:17 PM ADT
To: mom4@aol.com

The Pirates are still Plundering and Pillaging. They make

us stay in the Game Room a lot, which is BO RING but I get to help sometimes. Estelle too. She is fun for a girl. All the other kids are cry babies. Mean while I hope a storm doesn't come because the Pirates are not very good at sailing the ship. Its zigging and zagging but Ali doesn't care. He is captain now. I just wish it had sails. Unc is still locked in the Casino with the other old men. They are all crying for mercy and stuff. I have a new friend named Claude. He gave me his Johnny Depp mask. He was in the French Foreign Legion but he's German. As dad would say, Go Figure! Love—

From: yohoho@africanprincess.com
Subject: PIRATE LORE
Date: August 3, 2007 10:11 AM ADT
To: bugdude@yahoo.com

Yo Bug

Guess what I have a Gameboy! This one boy, Vernon wouldnt stop crying so the Pirates put a plastic bag over his head. Pirates dont like cry babys. I don't blame them, who does? He was looking at me like crazy when he aspired and I just said Game Over and they all laughed even though they dont know English. Maybe they know a little. They gave me his GameBoy! But the batteries are all ready dead, just my luck. Estelle says HLO. She wants to meat you when this is over. I told her all about you, not everything tho! She tried to kiss me again. She likes Pirate stuff to. She thinks she is so cute in her bathing suit.:)

From: yohoho@africanprincess.com
Subject: PIRATE LORE
Date: August 3, 2007 2:24 PM ADT
To: mom4@aol.com

Hi Mom

Remember last Christmas when dad said somebody should put Aunt Bea out of her misery, and you all laughed because I thought he said mystery? Well anyway the pirates did. I went down to the cabin to get some batteries for my GameBoy and she was all cut up in peaces. They found her hiding place. Most of her fingers were gone but one. They left one ring and I saved it for you as a souvenir of Pirate Week. I have a GameBoy now.

From: yohoho@africanprincess.com
Subject: BATTLE ALERT
Date: August 4, 2007 6:29 PM ADT
To: bugdude@yahoo.com

Yo Bug

Today was the best! 3 helcopters came and buzzed around while the Pirates waved their guns at them. 2 were from TV and the other was Navy with duble rotors. There was a battle with machine guns and every thing. One of the Pirates was cut in 2 like a saw. Then one of the Pirates had a rocket thing and shot down the Navy helcopter. It spun around just like in Black Hawn Down, burning and everything! As soon as it hit the water, they started swimming out and the Pirates shot them in the water. That was fun. Claude even let me use his gun. It kicks so bad I fell backward and the Pirates all laughed. Im getting used to there cruel humor. Claude helped me up and showed me how to brace the gun against a railing. He's pretty nice for a Pirate. He has all gold teeth, completely. I only hit one pilot for sure. He was the last one and the Pirates left him for me. He was in a life jacket so he floated even after I shot his arms both off. Then the sharks came. It was getting dark so we went inside. Estelle wanted to shoot but they wouldn't let her. Claude shook my hand and gave me a cigarette. I only pretended to enhale. I don't want to get hooked. Unc says it only takes one.

From: yohoho@africanprincess.com
Subject: PIRATE WEEK
Date: August 5, 2007 3:11 PM ADT
To: mom4@aol.com

Hi Mom

I saw 2 helcopters this morning! One of them was Navy and one was TV. I think they are planning a Rescue. They flew around the ship a while. The pirates shot at them but they didnt shoot back because of the hostages in the deck chairs. Most of them are dead but the helcopters cant tell! The Pirates are very clever. Plus, they shot down one helicopter. It spun down just like in the movie and then the pilots swam out and then the Pirates shot them in the water, and then the sharks came. Then the Pirates shot at the sharks to! I think that was mean since sharks are undangered. They are harder to kill then people tho. I hope the helcopters come back but then Pirate Week will be over. I miss you and Dad.

From: yohoho@africanprincess.com
Subject: PIRATE LORE
Date: August 5, 2007 6:43 PM ADT
To: bugdude@yahoo.com

Yo Bug

These Pirates are not very good at sailing. The ship is going in circles. I can tell by looking at the wake, thats the bubbles out behind. Were going to slow to get dizzy tho. The sharks are in the bubbles eating the dead bodies which float. Its like a picnic for them. They would probably get dizzy if they were not fish. Its pink like a rainbow in spots. Estelle from Joeburg says HLO. One of them is her step father she thinks. Look for us on TV! More later

From: yohoho@africanprincess.com
Subject: PIRATE LORE
Date: August 6, 2007 1:34 PM ADT
To: mom4@yahoo.com

Hi Mom

Unc was on TV! The helicopters buzzed around this morning while the Pirates threw some of the men overboard. There putting on quite a show! First they tie them together back to back, so they cant swim. I wish they would make them walk the plank but there is no plank. Anyway Unc was in the first batch. Hes so fat that he floated on top and the other guy drowned first. Then the sharks hit from both sides at once and that was cool, like Sea World. I can still see his crazy shirt that you gave him. Maybe a shark is wearing it! He and Aunt Bea will sure have some crazy stories to tell when Pirate Week is over!

From: yohoho@africanprincess.com
Subject: PIRATE LORE
Date: August 7, 2007 2:41 PM ADT
To: bugdude@yahoo.com
Yo Bug

Guess what I am the only kid left. Estelle and I were watching the sharks and she is always trying to hold my hand. I pushed her away and then Claude pulled down her bathing suit to show her tittys, and the Pirates all laughed because they were so small. I felt sorry for her but then she started to cry and she knew that would make them mad. Ali asked me if she was my girl friend and I said No Way. I guess Yes was the right answer but I wasnt thinking fast. Claude started up the chainsaw and cut her hand off and threw it overboard. They made her watch the sharks eat it. Then they let her go but she died anyway. She didn't say anything first. That was kind of sad and Im all alone now in the Game Room. Some Game Room! I hope she wont be mad at me when Pirate Week is over. She has a temper tho. You will see when you meat her!

From: yohoho@africanprincess.com
Subject: PIRATE LORE
Date: August 7, 2007 5:15 PM ADT
To: mom4@aol.com
Yo Mom

I have the Game Room all to my self. All the other kids are dead, even Estelle. They are in a pile in the corner. It doesn't smell so good any more. This Gameboy is cool tho, I hope I get to keep it when Pirate Week is over. The batteries are mine anyway. They are from Aunt Beas hair do thing. Well good night from your loving son—

From:	yohoho@rsamandela.com
Subject:	PIRATE LORE
Date:	August 8, 2007 10:19 AM ADT
To:	mom4@aol.com

Hi mom

Good news! I have been rescued. It was scary at first but only for awhile. I fell asleep at the computer last night and when I woke up all the Pirates were gone. It was awful quiet and when I ran out there were just a few dead people left on the decks. It was kind of sad after all the Plundering and Pillaging, like at the movie when the show is over and everybody stands up. The ship was leaning pretty bad and it was hard to walk, but I held on to the rail. There were still a lot of fingers and stuff. Pirates never clean up! The front of the ship was burning and the smoke smelled like hair, so I went to the back to wait, called the stern. Sure enough, the helcopters came back, and a boat too. The sailers wore sailer suits and they told me I was a hero. Two of them wore wet suits. My picture will be in the paper I bet. Im writing this from the computer room in the Navy ship. There going to bring me home on a Navy helcopter!

From:	yohoho@rsamandela.com
Subject:	PIRATE LORE
Date:	August 8, 2007 6:09 PM ADT
To:	cooldude@yahoo.com

Yo Bug

Im writing this from the computer room in the Navy ship. Its like the Game Room only better. You wouldnt believe the stuff they have! The Navy guys are nice but I like the Pirates better. The greaf countsler took my necklace away but it was turning black anyway. She let me keep my Pirate hat. I didnt show her Curtises nose in my pocket. She has been trying to make me cry. No luck so far! ☺

From:	yohoho@rsamandela.com
Subject:	PIRATE WEEK
Date:	August 9, 2007 10:31 AM ADT
To:	mom4@aol.com

I will see you at the Capetown airport tomorrow. Tell dad to come to. My greaf countsler says I am a survivor. Thats like a hero. Well all be on TV so tell dad to come to. Ill wear my Pirate hat and the Johnny Depp mask that Claude gave me. Tell Unc and Aunt Bea thanks if you see them before I do. Im sorry they didnt have fun. I could tell they didnt. Wait till you see my Gameboy. Your loving son—

"Captain Jack Sparrow" (Yo ho ho)

The Stamp

Everybody collects something, even if it's only stamps. Or dreams.

Orville collected stamps. His big brother, Wilbur, collected dreams.

That made it hard to know what to get Wilbur for his birthday. He would be twelve soon.

Then Orville saw the magazine. *WONDER TALES for BOYS*. The perfect thing for a dreamer!

"Happy Birthday," he said.

Wilbur loved it. It was filled with stories about submarines and flying machines. He hoped he could get his little brother, Orville, something half so nice. He would be eight in a few months.

Wilbur looked through the little ads in the back of the magazine. They were for novelties of all kinds: invisible ink, handshake buzzers, secret signal whistles.

Then he saw the ad for STAMPS FROM THE FUTURE.

"Perfect," he said to himself. He ordered them for Orville's birthday—which was in the future, after all!

They came just in time. "Happy birthday," Wilbur said.

☆　☆　☆

Orville tried to hide his disappointment. He only liked real stamps, and these were just gag fakes. Plus there were only four of them.

One stamp showed a man called Elvis. He was pouting like a girl.

Another showed a Negro with a baseball bat. Nobody ever put Negroes on stamps.

Another was of a woman without a crown. Real stamps only showed women when they were queens.

Another showed...

"Hey, this is neat!" said Orville. Suddenly he was excited. "How did you do this?"

"Do what?" asked Wilbur.

Orville handed him the stamp. It showed two grown men in stiff collars with a box kite behind them.

The two men looked familiar.

Underneath them, it said: The Wright Brothers.

"This," said Orville.

"I didn't do it," said Wilbur. "I just sent for STAMPS FROM THE FUTURE. It was a novelty ad. I didn't tell them what to send."

"Maybe they're really from the future," said Orville. His voice sounded spooky.

"That's impossible," said Wilbur.

Orville shrugged. "You always told me that nothing was impossible," he said. "Maybe you and I are famous in the future."

"Don't be silly," said Wilbur. "For what?"

☆ ☆ ☆

Then Wilbur looked at the stamp more closely.

There was a man lying flat on the box kite behind the grown-up Wilbur and Oliver. He was flying through the air.

Maybe I was right, thought Wilbur. Maybe nothing is impossible, after all.

"I can't wait to show this to my friends," said Orville.

"Not yet," said Wilbur. "Put it away for a few years. You and I have work to do."

Catch 'Em in the Act

Lou was almost thirty. He had a job and an apartment, but he was lonely. He didn't have any friends. He didn't know why; he just didn't.

So he did what everyone who is lonely does: YouTube and eBay. One day it was eBay.

"Say, look at this!" he murmured. Lou often murmured to himself.

CRIMESTOPPERS™ VIDEO CAMERA
Catch 'em in the Act!
BUY IT NOW: 19.95
Brand New in Box.
Batteries Included.
One to a Customer
Shipping, 4.99

That didn't seem like all that much. The shipping wasn't bad either. That's usually where they get you. So Lou did what every lonely person with PayPal does. He clicked on BUY.

Four days later, it came. It was about the size of a cell phone, with a little viewscreen that folded out to one side.

It only had two buttons: SHOOT and PLAY. Not a lot of features. But the price was right.

Lou pointed it at his cat and looked in the viewscreen.

There was the cat. The picture in the viewscreen was black and white, with a little Date&Time display at the top. It was even grainy, like a real surveillance video.

Cool! Lou pressed SHOOT.

The cat took a crap in the corner, and then left the room, looking like a criminal. But cats always look like criminals.

Lou pressed PLAY. There it was again in the viewscreen: the cat, the crap, the corner, in grainy black and white, with Date&Time at the top: **04/18/2008/8:44 p.m.**

The cat slunk off and the screen went blank.

Lou hit PLAY and watched it again.

"Cool," he murmured.

It was time to try it out in the real world. There was a Seven-Eleven only blocks away.

It was empty. Lou went in and wandered to the back of the store. He looked through the viewscreen and scanned the scene, from the beer case in the back to the Pakistani clerk reading a magazine behind the counter. He looked pretty bored.

Lou hit SHOOT. The Pakistani clerk looked up from his magazine toward the cash register. He hit NO SALE and took a bill out the cash register and stuck it in his shirt pocket. **04/18/2008/8:58 p.m.**

Lou hit PLAY and watched him do it again. It was a five.

Cool, thought Lou. He looked around the store through the viewscreen. In grainy black and white, with the Date&Time display, it looked like a crime scene. But Seven-Elevens all look like crime scenes. What it needed was more people.

A black guy came in for Salems and a lottery ticket. Lou got him in the viewscreen and was just about to press SHOOT when the black guy turned and looked straight at him.

"Hey, asshole!" he said. "What the fuck are you doing?"

"Nothing," said Lou. "Making a call." He pretended to be punching in a number.

"Somebody ought to kick your ass," said the black guy. He paid and left. The clerk went back to his magazine. It was *People*. Lou pretended to be looking for something in the candy aisle.

A fat white kid came in. Lou knew him. It was the kid from upstairs over Lou's apartment. He was about twelve. He lived with his mother. Lou wasn't afraid of him.

Through the viewscreen, in black and white, with the Date&Time display, the kid looked like a perp. He went straight to the candy aisle and picked out a Snickers.

Lou pressed SHOOT and watched the kid approach the counter. Instead of paying for the candy bar he stuck it into his jacket pocket. Then he jammed it forward like a gun. **04/18/2008/9:04 p.m.**

"Open the fuckin' register," he said. "Give me the bills. Keep the change. Keep your hands in sight or I'll blow you away."

"OK, OK!"

The Pakistani clerk opened the cash register and took out a wad of bills. He handed it to the kid, who backed out the door, still with his hand jammed in his pocket. **04/18/2008/9:05 p.m.**

Then he ran.

"Did you see that?" asked the clerk. Lou shrugged and said, "Not really." He didn't want to get involved.

He backed out the door and left the Pakistani clerk calling the cops. He went back to his apartment and pressed PLAY.

There was the fat kid, robbing the store. It had the Date&Time and everything.

Lou watched it several times. He liked crime videos.

The next day after work Lou went by the fat kid's apartment. It was right upstairs. He waited until he was sure the mother was away.

"What do you want?" the fat kid asked. He didn't want to open the door.

"I saw you rob the Seven-Eleven," Lou said.

The fat kid opened the door. "You're a liar," he said. But he didn't sound like he was sure.

Lou hit PLAY and showed him the video on the viewscreen. "I didn't mean to," the fat kid said. "I don't know what came over me."

"That's what they all say," said Lou. "Give me half the money or I will call the police."

The fat kid gave him half the money. "Let me see that thing," he said, pointing at the video camera.

"No way," said Lou. He went home and counted the money. It was $62, more than he made in a week.

The next day, Lou called in sick. "I have the flu," he said. His boss grumbled but didn't say anything.

Lou took his new Crimestoppers™ video camera to the mall. It was almost empty during the day. There was only one girl shopping. She was extremely pretty.

In the viewscreen she looked like a perp.

Cool, thought Lou.

He followed her up the escalator to Level Two. He watched her in the viewscreen as she went into Cinderella's Slipper, a shoe store. He pressed SHOOT. She picked up a pair of socks when the clerk wasn't looking and stuck them down into her tanktop.

Lou followed her to the food court. She got a taco salad. He sat down at the table with her even though all the other tables were empty.

"Beat it," she said. "I'm calling Security."

"I have something to show you," said Lou. He set the video camera on the table, unfolded the viewscreen, and pressed PLAY. There she was, stealing the socks at **04/19/2008/10:14 a.m.**

"I don't know what came over me," she said.

"That's what they all say," said Lou. "I'm calling the cops unless you split the loot with me."

The girl just laughed. "What are you going to do with one sock?"

That was a good question. "Keep 'em both, then," said Lou. "Think of me as a friend." She was extremely pretty.

"Not even a remote possibility," said the girl, her mouth full. "I don't like your style. Plus, you are not all that good looking."

"What style?" asked Lou.

"Plus, my mother is picking me up," she said, scooting back from the table. It, but not the chair, was bolted to the floor. Lou followed her, at a safe distance, out to the parking lot. Her mother was waiting in a Lexus. Lou watched in the viewscreen as the pretty girl got in and slammed the door.

He pressed SHOOT as the Lexus drove off. It scraped the side of a Hyundai on the way out of the parking lot, but didn't stop.

Lou went home alone. He watched his crime videos and then went to bed. Now he had two. But he still didn't have any friends.

The next day Lou called in sick again.

"This is getting old," said his boss.

"It's the bird flu," said Lou. He had $62 and he knew how to get more.

He went to the bank. It was a branch with only one teller. He watched the customers come in and out, then picked out a little old lady with a shopping bag. He got her in the viewscreen and pressed SHOOT.

She pulled a ski mask and a .44 out of the shopping bag. She put on the ski mask and fired the gun into the ceiling. **04/20/2008/09:18 a.m.**

Everybody hit the floor.

"Hand it over, motherfucker!" the little old lady yelled. The teller filled her shopping bag with money, and she ran out the door.

Lou followed her.

She ripped off her ski mask and jumped onto a bus.

Lou jumped on behind her. He sat down beside her even though all the other seats were empty.

"I saw you rob that bank," he said.

"No, you did not!" she said. She was out of breath.

"Yes, I did," said Lou. He pressed PLAY and showed

her the viewscreen and she shook her head in amazement. "I don't know what came over me," she said.

"That's what they all say," said Lou. He made her give him half the money. It was $560, more than he made in a month. It was all in twenties.

He got off at the next stop and went home and watched crime videos. Now he had three. The cat walked through the room, prancing like a criminal, but Lou ignored it. He didn't want to run down the batteries.

The next day Lou called in sick again.

"This is getting old," said his boss. "You are fired."

Lou didn't give a damn and told him so. He had $622. What did he need with a job?

He went back to the mall. The pretty girl was there again. Her mother apparently dropped her off every day. There was hardly anybody else around.

Lou followed her up the escalator. He watched her in the viewscreen as she walked into Cinderella's Slipper. He pressed SHOOT. She swiped a pair of little pink socks and stuck them down into her tanktop. It was pink too. Then she went to the food court and ordered a taco salad. Lou sat down beside her.

"I warned you," she said. "I'm calling Security."

"Go ahead, they might be interested in seeing this," said Lou. He showed her the video of her stealing the socks at **04/21/2008/10:22 a.m.**

"I told you, I don't know what came over me," she said.

"I do," said Lou. He explained to her about the

Crimestoppers™ video camera. "Everybody that I shoot commits a crime," he said. "They can't help it."

"It must be magic," she said. "If so, it's not evidence."

"There's no such thing as magic," said Lou. "It could be from another dimension, or something. I got it on eBay." He made her look at the video again.

"It's not evidence anyway," she said. "The socks are pink and that's in black and white."

"I'm not interested in turning you in anyway," said Lou. "I just want to make friends."

"You have a funny way of going about it," said the pretty girl. "Now if you will excuse me, my mother is picking me up."

Lou followed her out to the parking lot and watched her on the viewscreen getting into the Lexus. He pressed SHOOT. On its way out of the lot the Lexus ran over a little dog but didn't stop.

Lou went home alone. He was more lonely than ever.

☆   ☆   ☆

That night he was watching crime videos when there was a knock at the door.

It was the fat kid. The little old lady was with him.

"How did you find me?" Lou asked.

"There are ways," said the little old lady.

"Let's see that thing," the fat kid said.

"What thing?" Lou asked.

"You know what thing," they both said.

Lou showed them the Crimestoppers™ video camera and explained to them how it worked. "Everybody I shoot commits a crime," he said. "They just can't help it."

"You're telling me!" said the little old lady.

"That's why we're here," said the fat kid. It turned out they both had enjoyed the experience, and now they wanted to form a criminal gang. "Your apartment will be our hideout," said the little old lady. "You can be our boss," said the kid.

Lou wasn't so sure. But he let them stay. He even let them play with the cat. He was lonely and a criminal gang was better than nothing.

The next day Lou called in sick again. Then they went downtown and committed some crimes. They stole a box of nails at the hardware store and a thousand dollars at the Indian casino. Then they went back to their hideout and divided up the loot.

"That video camera is cool," said the fat kid as they divided up the loot. "It's like magic."

"It's apparently from another dimension," said Lou.

"Dimension shimension," said the little old lady. "It's from the future if you ask me."

"I got it on eBay," said Lou. He was beginning to worry about the batteries.

The next day Lou called in sick again. "You don't work here anymore," said his boss. "So knock off the damn calling in."

They went downtown and committed more crimes. Then they went back to their hideout and divided up the loot. Then Lou and the fat kid watched crime videos while the little old lady played with the cat.

Lou had $979.12 by now but he couldn't get the pretty girl off his mind.

"Why the long face?" the fat kid asked.

"Fess up, Boss," said the little old lady.

Lou showed them the crime video of the pretty girl at the mall. He told them everything but the truth: that he wanted her as his girlfriend. He had only just realized it himself.

"She's a skillful one, that one," said the little old lady.

"I'll bet that Lexus is filled with socks!" said the fat kid. "We should ask her to join our criminal gang."

"Hmmmm," murmured Lou. He was beginning to come up with a plan.

☆   ☆   ☆

The next day Lou called in sick again. He hung up as soon as his boss answered. Then they all went to mall together. They got there late. The pretty girl was already in the food court, having a taco salad.

Her tank top looked stuffed with socks.

"You again," she said, when she looked up and saw Lou approaching, watching her on his tiny viewscreen. "You're wasting your time. How can I commit a crime while I'm eating my lunch? Brunch. Whatever."

It was **04/23/2008/10:09 a.m.** She didn't see the little old lady and the fat kid sneaking up behind her. Lou pressed SHOOT and they immediately went to work kidnapping her. They duct taped her to her chair and gagged her so she couldn't scream for help.

They carried her on the chair to Lou's apartment, which was now their hideout.

"What's the big idea?" she asked, as soon as the gag was removed.

Lou explained to her about the criminal gang. "We want you to join," he said. He introduced his two partners. He didn't use their real names, which he didn't know anyway.

"You're a natural," said the little old lady. "We steal a lot more than socks," said the fat kid.

"There is no way I'm joining your criminal gang," the girl said, looking at Lou with scorn. "I already told you, I don't like your style. And you're not all that good looking. So untie me. Or untape me. Whatever."

"Only if you will join our criminal gang," said Lou. "Otherwise, you are a hostage. Your call," he added.

Before she could reply yes or no, he got her in the viewscreen and pressed SHOOT.

"OK, I will join your criminal gang," she said. "And I will be your girlfriend, too." It was **04/23/2008/12:19 p.m.**

"What's this about a girlfriend?" asked the little old lady.

"But my mother is picking me up in the mall parking lot at one o'clock," the pretty girl added. "I have to tell her I won't be coming home again or otherwise she will worry."

"Fair enough," said Lou.

"Don't trust her!" said the fat kid.

But Lou was the boss. They carried her on the chair to the mall parking lot and untaped her just as her mother was pulling in. But instead of telling her mother that she was never coming home again, so she wouldn't worry, the girl jumped into the Lexus and rolled down the power window.

"Fuck you and your criminal gang!" she shouted as they sped off.

Lou watched her depart with tears in his eyes. He didn't even bother to shoot her departure.

"Told you," said the fat kid.

"Why the two sad faucets?" asked the little old lady when they got back to the hideout. Lou was crying. "This kidnapping was a bust, but there are lots of other crimes waiting to be committed," she said, trying to cheer him up.

"The day is yet young," said the fat kid. "So 'fess up, Boss, why the long face?"

In a sudden burst of honesty that surprised even himself, Lou explained that it wasn't the crime of kidnapping that had interested him, but the victim herself—the pretty girl.

"I feel used," said the little old lady, the cat on her lap.

The fat kid was crying himself. "What about our criminal gang?"

Lou confessed that it wasn't the criminal gang he had wanted all along but a girlfriend. He didn't give a damn about the criminal gang.

"You devious bastard!" said the fat kid. He went off on Lou. Then he reached into the little old lady's shopping bag and pulled out the .44.

"Careful with that," said the little old lady. "It's a one-way ticket to Hell."

"Good!" said the fat kid. He pointed the gun at Lou but he couldn't pull the trigger no matter how hard he tried.

"I've got an idea," said the little old lady. She grabbed the video camera from Lou and pointed it at the fat kid.

She got him in the viewscreen and pressed SHOOT. "Try it again," she said.

"No," said Lou.

"Yes!" BLAM! The fat kid pulled the trigger and fired at Lou but missed, just barely. The bullet went through the cat and then demolished the computer at **04/23/2008/01:32 p.m.**

"Try again," said the little old lady. She pressed SHOOT again. But just as the fat kid was pulling the trigger, the viewscreen went blank.

She handed it back to Lou.

"The batteries are dead," he said. He was sorry, yet relieved.

"Bummer," said the little old lady. She took her .44 back and dropped it into her shopping bag. It wasn't real anymore; it hardly weighed anything.

A silence fell over the hideout. The cat was bleeding to death.

"What now, boss?" asked the fat kid. Lou was in charge again.

They took the Crimestoppers™ video camera to Walgreens and showed it to the clerk.

"It takes Triple Es," said the clerk. "The problem is, there's no such thing. It must be from another galaxy or something."

"Then I guess that's it," said the fat kid dejectedly. "That's the end of our criminal gang."

"I should have know it would never last," said the little old lady. "I'm outa here."

"You and me both," said the fat kid, and they left, but

not together. Each went to his or her own home. The criminal gang was *kaput*.

"Good riddance," murmured Lou. He wasn't going to miss those two. But now he felt more alone than ever.

"Can I help you with something else?" asked the clerk.

Lou couldn't think of anything so he just went home.

Lou called in sick the next day.

"I told you, you don't work here anymore," said his boss. "Quit calling."

Lou went to the mall. There was the pretty girl again. She pretended to ignore him. He followed her up the escalator to Cinderella's Slipper and watched her steal a pair of socks. Without the video camera, she got caught. Her father made her give them back. It turned out that he was the store owner. Lou went to the food court and waited for her to show up.

"I'm sorry about the kidnapping," he said. "I just wanted a girlfriend. The criminal gang thing is over. *Kaput.*"

"Too late," she said. "I hated that tape."

"You did say OK, you would be my girlfriend," Lou reminded her.

"I don't know what came over me," she said with a mean smile. "That was on your Crimestoppers™ video and perps always lie."

"How about I buy you lunch," Lou suggested. He still had his $979.12. It was burning a hole in his pocket.

"If you insist," she said. "You're not all that bad looking." Lou felt a momentary stirring of hope that perhaps things were going to work out after all. She picked out a taco salad. It was only $6.25, but when Lou pulled out a twenty to pay, the cashier held it up to the light. "This is counterfeit," he said. "I'm calling the police."

"I should have known," said the pretty girl.

"It's the batteries," said Lou, showing her the dead video camera. "Without them, crime doesn't pay."

"So, replace them," she said.

Lou explained the problem. "It takes triple E's," he said, "and there's no such thing."

"It must be from some alien planet," said the girl. "I never liked your style anyway."

Then she walked away, prancing like a cat, leaving the unbought taco salad behind. Lou didn't follow her. It was over, he could tell. He could hear sirens. He walked home alone.

His apartment was lonelier then ever. It felt more like a hideout than a home. Not only did Lou not have a girlfriend, he didn't have a job anymore. His money was worthless. His Crimestoppers™ video camera was no good anymore and it was one to a customer. His computer was totally demolished and to top it all off, his cat was dead. That one shot had done it in.

The police were pulling up out front. The pretty girl was with them. She had apparently led them to his hideout.

Lou locked the door and sat with the dead cat on his lap. Its fur was still soft in places. Soon he felt better. "So what," he murmured to himself. So what if he had failed, and he had to admit he had. Nothing ventured, nothing gained.

04/24/2008/02:47 p.m. The police were breaking down the door but Lou would never forget his adventures with the Crimestoppers™ video camera. And he had learned an invaluable life-lesson. Now at least he knew what the problem was.

It had something to do with his style.

A Special Day

The immense lobby was almost empty. It was a Monday, after all, not a big day for tourists.

"Oh, Honey, where did you get that?"

"I picked it, Mom. Isn't it pretty?"

"Yes, but you aren't supposed to pick them."

"It's OK," said an older man in a full-dress fireman's uniform, who was waiting for the elevator with them. "It's a daisy."

"Isn't it pretty?"

"It's a doozy of a daisy," the fireman agreed with a sad smile.

"Please excuse her," said the little girl's mother. "We're visiting from Indiana and this is our first trip to New York City."

"Welcome, then. Ladies first!"

The doors opened and they all crowded into the car: a little girl and her mother in bright pastels, followed by a sad-faced fireman; then two young men in jeans, an older man in Arab dress, a Marine in uniform, and a lawyer in an Italian suit.

"Step to the rear of the car, folks," said the elevator operator, a gray-haired woman of sixty-five.

The little girl stared at the Arab. "Why is he wearing a dress, Mom?"

"It's not a dress, he's a foreigner. Now hush!"

"It's OK."

"You speak English?"

"I went to Indiana University."

"No kidding! We're from Indiana."

"So I overheard. And since you were kind enough to ask, young lady, I'm wearing this dress because I'm an Imam. That's an Islamic cleric."

"Like a preacher?" asked the little girl.

"Bingo," he said. "Very like."

"I'm a Catholic priest myself," said the fireman, extending a hand. "Partners in crime, as it were."

"Cleverly disguised as a fireman?" said the Imam with a smile.

"NYFD Chaplain. I'm on a kind of a ceremonial mission here today. That accounts for the full dress get-up."

"Watch the closing doors," said the operator.

The elevator started up.

The two young men at the back held hands silently. The Marine stood beside them stiffly, as if at attention. The lawyer in the Italian suit stared curiously at the elevator operator.

The little girl covered her ears.

"My ears hurt!" she said.

"That's because we're going up very fast," said the operator. "Almost a thousand feet so far. We'll stop at the 78th floor and you will change elevators. That one will take you to—"

The elevator stopped with a sickening *bump*. The lights went out.

"Mommy, it's dark!"

"What happened?" her mother asked, alarmed.

"Not to worry," said the operator, with a thick New York accent. She got on the phone. "It's a power failure, temporary. They say it'll be ten minutes."

"It's dark, Mommy!"

"Don't worry, little girl," said the priest disguised as a fireman. He found her shoulder with his hand. "Perhaps we should introduce ourselves, to pass these few minutes till we are moving again. Have you ever made friends in the dark before?"

There was no answer.

"I am Father Mychal Judge, but you can call me Father Mike."

"Imam Habib," said the Imam. "Visiting your beautiful city from Baghdad."

"Another beautiful city," said Father Mike. "And an ancient one. The cradle of civilization."

"You are welcome in the cradle at any time," said the Imam. "It's a World Heritage site now, you know."

"I been there," said a rich black voice from the back of the car. "I was assigned to the UN Friendship Force sent to help in the Restoration."

"An exemplary mission," said the Imam, finding the Marine's hand in the dark and shaking it. "Especially since so many here, as well as there, were so eager to loose the Dogs of War. And your name, young man?"

"Washington, Caleb, Master Sergeant, USMC. Proud native of Harlem, USA."

"My brother's a Marine," said the little girl's mother. "I'd be proud to shake your hand, if I could find it."

"A pleasure, ma'am."

"Ouch!"

"Sorry ma'am. Guess I'm a little nervous. Don't mind choppers but don't much like elevators."

The elevator operator made another call. "They're working on it," she said. "Thank you for your patience."

It was very dark. In the distance, they could hear an alarm bell.

"I'm not afraid," said the little girl. "I'm five."

"I was five once," said Father Mike. "Long long ago."

They all laughed. It made a nervous sound in the crowded elevator.

"I believe you mentioned a ceremonial mission," said the Imam, restarting the conversation.

"Yes, yes, of course," said Father Mike. "I come here once a year to bring a few flowers. And to say a prayer from the highest point in our city. It's a personal ceremony, to honor the firefighters that we lost in the past year."

"That's lovely," said the mother.

"Not so lovely this year, I'm afraid," said Father Mike. "We lost eight this year. That's a lot."

"I'm sorry," said the Imam. "But why September?"

"I come every year on September eleventh. Nine eleven, nine-one-one. It's sort of symbolic. Emergency number. I knew these boys."

There was a long silence. The operator made another call. "They're working on it," she said.

"Thank you for not thanking us for our patience again," said Father Mike, trying to lighten the mood.

No one laughed.

It was awfully dark.

"You two are awfully quiet," said the Imam, speaking into the darkness. "Where are you from?"

"Beirut, Imam," answered a shy voice. "But we're not Lebanese. I'm Ali, I'm Palestinian. Ben here is Israeli."

"Romeo and Julio," said Ben with a laugh. "And we're here on a sort of ceremonial mission too. Nine eleven is also our special day."

"Oh, really," said Father Mike. He was hoping for more, but there was just a long dark silence.

It was broken by the elevator operator.

"I believe we have a lawyer with us," she said. "Perhaps he'd like to testify."

Another voice came from the darkness, with a slight Spanish accent: "She is right, I'm that dread creature, a lawyer. The name is Al. I'm from Texas, in New York working with the Human Rights Commission of the UN."

"The new anti-torture protocols," said the operator. "That's good work, and about time."

"How did you know about that? And how did you know I'm a lawyer?"

She laughed. "Your shoes. I'm a lawyer too."

"Operating an elevator? Not that…"

"Not that there's anything wrong with that," quipped Father Mike.

"It's sort of a special assignment. About a dozen years ago, some misguided souls tried to blow up this very building, and I defended them. A little too vigorously, perhaps."

"Lynne Stewart!" the lawyer said. "I thought you looked familiar. I signed the petition in your case. It was very unfair, trying to disbar you. But…"

"I'm doing community service. It's a penalty, but a rather enjoyable one."

"I admire your work," said the lawyer. "The General Amnesty especially. That got a lot of people out of prison."

"We met in prison," said Ali from the darkness. "Romeo here was a guard."

"And Julio was a prisoner," said Ben. "That was before the Peace Accords of course."

"And before the anti-torture protocols for sure," added Ali.

Fumbling in the darkness, they all shook hands, clumsily. "You'll have to excuse my left," Ben said. "Ali and I are holding hands all the way up. It's an essential part of our private ceremony."

"Oh, really?" said Father Mike. This time he was rewarded with an answer:

"Yes, five years ago, exactly, on nine-eleven, two thousand and one, we..."

"We're moving again!" squealed the little girl.

And indeed they were.

The lights came on. They all looked around at one another shyly, as if they had just met, which indeed they had.

The door opened onto the 78th floor skylobby.

"We're all one party now," said the lawyer, hesitating in the elevator door. "I wish you could join us at the top."

"We all have our work to do," said the operator with a smile. "The Up elevator is over there. This one's going down."

The top of the building was flooded with sunlight. The little girl ran and looked over the east side, at the tower's giant twin. Her mother and the Marine followed close behind.

The lawyer stood alone in the center. "I don't really care for heights," he said.

Father Mike walked to the north parapet, looking over

the city. He crossed himself and wiped away a tear. The Imam stood at his side. "Mind if I join you in a prayer?" he asked.

He didn't, and he did.

After a moment they joined Ali and Ben, who were looking out over the Hudson toward New Jersey to the west.

"You mentioned a ceremony," Father Mike said.

They were arm in arm, no longer holding hands.

"Five years ago today," said Ali, "we were in despair. We had run away to NY to be together but we couldn't forget our families, our people, all that strife and sorrow."

Ben looked around to make sure the little girl wasn't near. "We chose nine-eleven for the same reason you did. A call for help. We were going to end it all. We came up here to jump, and die hand in hand."

"God have mercy!" said Father Mike.

"He did," said Ali. "Just as we were about to step off a plane passed over. A 767. A most beautiful craft."

"Ali's an aeronautical engineer," explained Ben. "But even to me, it looked like an angel of mercy, reflecting the light. An angel of peace and world unity."

The Imam nudged him. The little girl was approaching.

"And you know the rest," finished Ali. "We decided to go home to the Middle East and work for peace."

"Courageous work," said the Imam. "Especially when so many there, as well as here, were so eager to loose the Dogs of War."

"Aren't you repeating yourself?" asked Father Mike. "Not that there's anything wrong with that."

The Imam shrugged extravagantly. "Religion is all about repetition."

"So is love," said Ben.

"Here." The little girl held out the daisy. "Mother said you were gay!"

Her mother, behind her, blushed.

"Daisies are gay too!"

"So they are," said Ali, taking the flower. He kissed her on the forehead and handed the daisy to Ben.

"Thank you," said Ben. "You never told us your name."

"It's Veronica. I'm five."

"You're the hope of the world, Veronica. Now let's give this daisy to the wind."

And he did.

"There's a lovely Irish bar on Chambers St," said Father Mike, pressing the *down* button. "I don't indulge these days, but I'd love to stand a round."

"I'm not a drinker," said the Imam. "But I'll come along and have a lemonade with the ladies."

"I like white wine," said the little girl's mother.

"I could stand a cold Harp," said the Marine.

"Ditto," said Ben and Ali, together.

"I picked up some cigars on my way through Havana last month," said the lawyer. He reached into his Italian suit and handed one to each of the men. "We can smoke in the bar, right?"

Father Mike rolled his eyes. "This *is* New York City!" he said.

"Here's the elevator!" said the little girl, whose name was Veronica.

Ali and Ben held hands all the way down.

BYOB FAQ

Where do you get your BOBs?
From you! Each and every BOB is unique, custom designed to order for each individual BYOB client. Your personal BOB, neurally mapped to your specs from an approved and tested BYOB blank, will be unique and like no other.

Are they really volunteers?
We wouldn't have it any other way. BYOB's program begins and ends with free choice, yours and his. BYOB's blanks are Asian and African males, ages 28-36, who have freely chosen to have their personalities erased and remapped (not just overwritten) in order to have a chance at a new life in the U.S. or Europe.

How are they selected?
With special care. *BYOB* accepts only healthy mature male blanks, HIV and STD clean, which are cosmetically and medically reconditioned before being neurally reconfigured to make a satisfactory boyfriend, life-partner or husband if you so desire.

How do you know what kind of guy I'm looking for?
You tell us. Simply *ENTER* your own needs, desires, likes, dislikes and preferences into our proprietary matching database. That's all there is to it! Unlike older programs, which matched people imperfectly, based on guesswork and

approximations, Build-Your-Own-Boyfriend lets you choose *exactly* the qualities you want in a life-partner. And then delivers it.

What if I don't speak computer-ese?

No problem. Our Personal Profile Mentor (PPP) prompts you through each of the twelve major neural networks seamlessly. You just list your own preferences, in your own words: Sense of humor? Does he like cats? Camping? Movies? Bob Dylan or Yanni? Is he the kind of guy who likes to cuddle on Sunday mornings? Your call. You tell BYOB exactly what you want, in plain English, then leave the rest to us.

Will he remember his previous life?

Your BOB comes with a full generic set of memories that is chemically dimmed, giving him a feeling of completeness without the specificity of individual recollection. You and your BOB will begin immediately making your own memories. That's what relationships are all about!

What about criminal tendencies?

Relax. While it is true that many of our blanks come from penal or military points of origin (POOs), they have been completely erased, not just overwritten, before reconfiguration. There is no such thing as a "criminal type," and even if there were, such tendencies would not survive BYOB's "deep cleansing" process. You can order a BOB with the full confidence that he will be a good citizen as well as a good companion.

What if he doesn't like me?
Unlikely, since your BOB is configured to like the same things you do—which includes yourself! And in the unlikely event that you are not satisfied (in every way) with your delivered BOB, you are free to return him at any time in the first six months after Reception, with only a nominal restocking fee and no questions asked. This happens in only a small percentage of cases.

What happens to rejected BOBs?
They are returned to inventory to be rewritten and reassigned. They have no memory of their reception. You have no responsibility for a returned blank.

Can I choose race or ethnicity?
Sorry. BYOB operates under strict non-discrimination laws. We guarantee only that your BOB will be healthy, pleasant looking with no disfigurements. Most are Asian or African, since EU restrictions prohibit European blanks at present.

Can I add Ls & Ds after delivery?
Of course! That's what relationships are all about. You and your BOB may discover birdwatching together, dabble in drag racing or explore the mysteries of tantric sex. Up to you! Your BOBs learning curve is matched to your own by our proprietary Neural Acquisition Protocol (NAP).

What if BYOB goes out of business?
Unlikely! Build-You-Own-Boyfriend (BYOB) has been providing life partners to busy career women for almost two

decades, with a documented satisfaction rate of 92.54 percent. We stand behind our services.

What if I don't want a long-term relationship?
Then our service is not for you. To adopt a metaphor from the stock market, we are not day traders, nor do we short-sell. BYOB is for the career woman willing to make an investment in a long-time partner. Have we mentioned that our BOBs have been reconditioned medically, and are covered by our Comprehensive Health Insurance policy (CHI)? You can and should look forward to a long and satisfying relationship.

Men only? What's that about?
We do service select gay men, but our service is primarily for women seeking a long-time companion or partner. Current international sex-traffic ordinances prevent our acceptance or reconfiguration of female blanks.

Will I have to teach him English?
Not at all. Your Bob comes with mature language capabilities, which are independent of memory. He may be teaching you, since our Syntax module is based on the Webster-Chomsky proprietary syntax map. He will however be unable to read or write. Many clients regard this as a plus.

Why only English?
Most of our clients are from English speaking countries, for cultural and religious reasons. Language underlays for French, German, and Spanish are in currently in development and are expected to be available soon.

What about accents?

Because our blanks are fully developed Asian and African men, they will come with accents ranging from slight to severe. Since intonation (accent) is muscular as well as neural, it diminishes after activation but never disappears entirely. Many women find this charming, and few find it an impediment to a lasting relationship.

What about citizenship?

Each BOB is awarded conditional citizenship six months after reception. It is among the many things he will be thankful to you for! And while BOBs cannot vote or own property, they have most of the rights of unconditional citizens. As an added attraction, Canadian or U.S. BYOB clients are granted an extra one-fifth vote. A similar concession is currently being negotiated with the British crown.

Will he long for his old life?

Certainly not. He will remember only that it was unpleasant and will be neurally incapable of remembering any specific incidents or people. His new life with you will be all that is of interest to him.

Will he know that he is a BOB?

Only if you tell him. He will know only that he has a past personality that he is disinclined (and indeed unable) to access. Many women find pleasure telling their BOBs that they have been especially designed to suit them. Many BOBs find comfort in the knowledge that they are "special" in this way. But again, it's your call.

Will he seek out other BOBs?

Probably not. Our studies show that BOBs in general have little interest in one another. His main interest will be in you, and he is configured to be more than satisfied with that.

What if I grow tired of him?

Why would you? Remember, your BOB wasn't just matched with you, he was made for you. But in the unlikely event that you wish to discard your BOB at any time after the initial BYOB warranty period, you can do so without legal prejudice by delivering him to Migration Control, since his citizenship is conditional and he is neurally mapped to go without resistance. Your responsibility then ends, and he free to become blanked again, or be returned to his Point of Origin (POO).

What if I have further questions?

They can be submitted in confidence to our BYOB website at www.Bob.bio; or if you wish to speak to a live operator, 1.919.456.8999. Now, may we ask *you* a question?

What are you waiting for?
Haven't you been lonely long enough?
Share your life with a BOB who is designed to fit
your life-style and unique personality.
Send for our Profile Initiator today—

Captain Ordinary

"It's a bird!" said a little boy.

"It's a plane!" said a little girl.

A man on the street looked up. A perfectly ordinary man, in tights and a cape. It was indeed a plane, trailing white smoke over the city.

"A biplane!" he muttered. "Can it be…"

It was. The summons he had long awaited. Even as he watched, the words began forming:

CALLING CAP

He didn't bother looking for a phone booth. They had all been hauled away years before. While everyone else on the street was watching the plane, he stripped off his tights, his cape…

CALLING CAPTAIN ORDINARY

And before the words were fully formed, there was a neatly-folded costume on the curb. If anyone looked down and saw a man in slacks and a sport coat standing in line at a nearby Starbucks, they thought nothing of it.

Nothing out of the ordinary in midtown New York.

Unnoticed by all except a select few, every third Starbucks has a narrow door between the broom closet and the unisex john/jane. Captain Ordinary's decaf soy latte order got him the key.

He felt a moment's claustrophobia as the rain-forest-free faux wood door clicked shut behind him, and then—

Nothing.

☆   ☆   ☆

Twelve hours later, Captain Ordinary was in abandoned quarry on the side of a remote Adirondack peak, passing his hand over the damp stone in a mystical pattern handed down for centuries. He stepped back, waiting for the door to lens open.

Nothing.

He rang the bell.

"Over here," said a bearded, tweedy figure, beckoning from a nearby cleft in the rock. "You're late."

"The teleporter was on the blink," Ordinary said, as he followed his host down the winding stairway into the bowels of the mountain. "I had to take the subway. Then the bus."

"Tell me about it," said Doctor Forever in the thick brogue that identified him as one of the Immortals charged with guarding humanity against extraordinary dangers. "The others are just now getting here themselves. There is no time to lose."

Captain Ordinary felt a thrill as he entered the electrically-lighted conference room and saw that the oval table was surrounded by familiar figures in colorful costumes. It wasn't every day that his leader and mentor assembled the entire Rad Pack of differently-abled emergency mutants from around the globe!

"I have dreadful news," said the dour Scot as he seated himself at the head of the table. "I have reason to believe that the Earth has been covered with some kind of Mundanity Shroud that renders us all powerless, more or less."

"Tell me about it," muttered Nano Man, groaning as he squeezed into his seat. His ability to make himself microscopic was the key to many of the Rad Pack's successful efforts. Full sized, he looked a little broad in the beam. Not to mention annoyed. "I suspected as much," said Rolex Girl, whose ability to travel backward as well as forward in time had proven so handy in the past. "My watch has stopped in the present."

"Something has slowed me down for sure," said Ftl, the bullet-headed dwrf, whose ability to outrun light itself had resulted in so many thrilling rescues. "I came at a trot. My Nikes are hardly warm."

"Where did this shroud come from?" asked Captain Ordinary, adjusting his balls in his slacks as he sat down at the table. "How can we overcome it?"

"First, we need a better look at it," said the gruff Scot, turning to Seti, whose gift for intimate contact with alien explorers had resulted in so many penetrating insights. "I was hoping that you could ask the Visitors to examine the Mundanity Shroud from the outside."

"I wish," Seti responded despondently, squirming on the donut-shaped cushion that he was never without. "I have been trying to contact those who probed me in the past, but without success. I'm beginning to wonder if it wasn't all a dream."

"This is bad!" said the tweedy Scot, beginning to look dismayed.

"What about the Hawking?" asked Captain Ordinary. "The interstellar spaceship that was dispatched several years ago to look for Earth-like planets among the distant stars? Perhaps that intrepid crew can look back at our planet and tell us what they see."

"I thought of that," said the immortal mentor, who was starting to sound shaky. "But they've all gone starkers from the smell on the ship. They began to lose it last month when methane ball futures went south. Plus it would take hours to get a message to them through the Shroud."

"Oh, dear," said Captain Ordinary. "It's that powerful?"

"It is apparently woven out of some kind of multi-dimensional superstring," the Hibernian groaned. "A tight weave indeed." Then, rallying his fading powers, he turned to the latest arrival, who was circling the table, having a hard time deciding where to sit.

"Quantum Gal, perhaps you can use your wormhole lens to get a better view. From an alternate but nearby universe, perhaps."

"I tried it on the way over," she said sadly. "All I can I see is a hole, with what looks like a worm at the bottom."

"Then all is lost," groaned the failing Scot. "This impenetrable Mundanity Shroud doubtless portends some awesome evil, I fear. And we are powerless against it."

"Power unless is awesome doom!" said a rasping, metallic, but welcome voice.

They all brightened. They had forgotten Aye Eye, the emotionless but brilliant computer intelligence that had constructed itself after a nuclear mishap and since given them so much crucial guidance.

Even Doctor Forever seemed encouraged. "What can you tell us, Aye Eye? Speak up, for God's sake!"

"Is God there no speak awesome," the digital conscious-ness droned dispassionately. "And is as does doom say ever."

"Gone bonkers," said the newly-dismayed Scot. "That's it, we're all done for, unless…" He closed his eyes and his chin dropped to his chest.

They all stared. "Unless what?" they all asked at once.

No answer.

"What's he thinking?" Ordinary asked Psi Guy, whose uncanny ability to read minds had proven so helpful in past crusades.

"Beats me. I have trouble reading my own mind these days, much less his."

"No wonder. He's dead," said Nano Man, who could tell by looking, even without microsizing and entering any of the expired Scot's several orifices.

"I thought he was immortal," said Rolex Girl disgustedly.

"Perhaps, in a way, he still is!" said Cyberboy, whose mutant ability to surf the matrix had shown them so many cybernetic shortcuts. The diminutive teen lifted the former Doctor Forever's gray ponytail and pulled a tiny device from the slot in the back of his thick neck. "Just for kicks," he said, "I downloaded our leader's brain into this flash drive."

The Rad Pack breathed a collective sigh of relief as Cyberboy stuck the flash drive under his tongue and sucked. But their hopes were dashed when he said, "System failure. All I'm getting is an error message: digital overload."

"Shit," said Rolex Girl.

"Bit of a problem," said Nano Man.

"We're fckd," said the dwrf.

"Not necessarily," said Captain Ordinary. He knew it was his job, as Control, to step up and take command. "I have a plan."

"What's that?" they all asked at once.

"Go home," he said. "Get a job. Get married. Have kids."

"I'm gay," said several.

"You can adopt," said Captain Ordinary. He was getting into the swing of it. His voice had a sudden ring of authority. "Take a break. Don't you deserve a rest after all you've done? Dress down. Live it up. Eat out. Watch TV. Mow the lawn. There are power mowers, you know. Take a course, learn physics…"

"Don't even think about it," said Quantum Gal, who was still circling the table, trying to decide which chair to take.

"…or form a book club," said Captain Ordinary. This was what he was here for. "Read Jane Austen or, better yet, Kim Stanley Robinson."

"Who's she?" they all asked at once.

Farewell Atlantis

I remember exactly when it all started, this incredible adventure. It was during *The Look of Love*, when she wakes up after the operation and sees her young doctor's face for the first time.

This guy sits down in the seat next to mine. "Hey," he says in a loud whisper.

"Sssk k kh!" I said. She was smiling and saying, "Because a woman sees with her heart, not her eyes."

"I need to talk to you."

"You're not supposed to talk in the movies."

"How do you know? Why not?"

"Just because," I said. This whole thing was making me nervous. I reached into my popcorn and he grabbed my wrist. It was my turn to say "Hey!" Nobody likes to be grabbed by a total stranger, especially at the movies.

He says, "Look at me," so I do.

"You look perfectly normal," I said, shaking his hand off my wrist. "So why don't you return to your seat before I get the usher."

"What usher?" he says. "Look around. Do you see anybody else in the theater at all?"

I looked around. It was a tiny theater, only about ten or twelve seats, and even in the dark I could see that all but ours were empty. The doctor was showing her flowers for the first time, so the bright colors made it easier.

"No," I said. "There was just the two of us. And you were sitting back there, where you belong."

"Why are there only twelve seats?"

"Beats me," I said, "Now may I watch the movie, please?" They were walking down Fifth Avenue. She was amazed at the sights. She had been blind all her life, until just yesterday.

"How come there's only one EXIT?" he whispered. "Aren't movie theaters supposed to have several? Something's not right!"

"Sk k kk k k," I said. They had just stopped in front of Tiffany's. She had never seen a diamond before.

"How come there's no concession stand? No lobby? No restrooms?"

"I already have popcorn," I said. I rattled the bag for proof. "And I never go to the restroom, I might miss something."

"Miss what?" he said. "How many movies have you seen since you've been here?"

"A lot. I don't count them. I just watch them."

"Do you remember buying a ticket? Do you remember sitting down? Do you remember anything before the movies?"

"No," I admitted. "Come to think about it, it is kind of peculiar."

"Now you are thinking about things!" He took my hand in his, and I let him hold it. "Stella," he said. "Something strange is going on here, and I won't rest until I figure out what it is."

His eyes were shining in the starlight (the doctor was showing her the stars) and suddenly he didn't look so crazy after all.

"How did you know my name?" I asked. "How come I know yours is Frank?"

"Beats me," he said, squeezing my hand. "But you are starting to wonder, to question things, and that's good." He stood up, pulling at me.

"Whoa," I said. "Where are we going?" I didn't want to lose my seat.

"The EXIT," said Frank. "I intend to try it, to see what is on the other side, come what may. But I can't do it—I can't do anything, apparently—without you by my side."

"Okay, okay," I said. Oddly enough, I was feeling the same way.

I grabbed my popcorn and followed him to the EXIT door, which was down beside the screen.

It opened with a little bar, which he knew how to operate.

It opened onto a metal corridor, studded with rivets. There was no street, no traffic, no town. I looked both ways to check.

"Just as I thought: we're in a spaceship," he said.

"That's absurd. It could be a submarine," I pointed out. "Or a cruise ship, like in *Loveboat*."

"Submarine corridors are narrower," Frank said. "Remember *Das Boot*? Two people could barely pass. And something tells me that this is no cruise we're on. Come on!"

I followed him for what seemed centuries. He hadn't brought his popcorn so we shared mine. The corridor was covered with moss, and vines popped out of the seams between the rivets. Sometimes we had to fight our way through them. There was rust everywhere.

"This ship, if it is a ship, is ancient," Frank said. "This leads me to think it's a starship, on a centuries-long journey. Remember *Destination: Arcturus?*"

I did, but just barely. We had come to a door that said STARSHIP COMMAND. And just in time. We were out of popcorn.

It opened with a little thumb device. It opened like a lens.

Frank stepped through and I followed. He had been right so far and I was beginning to trust him.

"Just as I suspected," he said. There were controls everywhere, dials and buttons and screens. On one side of the triangular room were twelve glass coffins in two rows of six.

Frank walked between them with slow steps, shaking his head. "Don't look, Stella," he said.

But I couldn't resist. Each held a mouldering corpse.

"The suspended animation must have failed," he said. "Except for these two."

The last two were empty, and open.

"Lucky for them," I said.

"Stella," Frank said, taking my hand, "Don't you get it? Those two are us! You and I are the only survivors. If this starship is on a mission to populate a new world, which I suspect it is, now it's up to us alone, you and me. We are Adam and Eve."

It was all beginning to make sense. "That must be why we are naked," I said. I had just noticed.

"And why you are so beautiful!" he said.

I covered up with my empty popcorn bag as best I could. He didn't even try.

"But first, there are important questions to answer," Frank went on excitedly. "What went wrong that the others all perished? And how did you and I survive the disaster? Who saved us? Who—or what?"

"Ship," said a deep robotic voice. It seemed to come from everywhere.

"Who are you?" Frank asked.

"I am Ship. It was my job to keep you all alive, but I guess I fell asleep. Luckily you two survived."

"Machines don't fall asleep," I pointed out.

"They do if they can't stay awake," said Ship. "I couldn't help it. I can barely keep my circuits open even now."

"*Try*," said Frank sternly. "We need some answers. How long have we been on this journey, Ship?"

"Six thousand years."

I gasped. That's a long time.

"That's six thousand of *my* years," said Ship. "Your years are of course very different from mine. I am a quantum device."

"How long in our years?" asked Frank.

"Five thousand, seven hundred and forty, point four."

"We've been watching movies for almost six thousand years?" I asked, amazed.

"No," said Ship. "You were in suspended animation, like the others, most of the time. You've only been watching movies, as you call them, for a week or so. It's the orientation period."

"Six thousand years is a damn long time," said Frank. "The Earth we left behind must be changed beyond all recognition. Our only hope is to push on to our destination. How long before we arrive?"

"You're there already," said Ship. "Parked in orbit. It was my job to open all twelve pods upon arrival and sleep-walk you to the theater for gradual awakening and orientation."

"That's why there were twelve seats!" said Frank.

"I fell asleep and ten of you died, as I said. I guess I should be ashamed."

"You *guess*?" I protested. He didn't sound ashamed.

Ship didn't answer. He had gone back to sleep.

"Some Ship," I said disgustedly.

"The two of us survived and that's the important part," said Frank. "Now it's our job to populate the new world that awaits us. I'm looking forward to it." He gave my hand a little squeeze.

I looked around. The control room didn't look very romantic.

"Not here, Stella, not now," he reassured me. "First we have to find out where we are, and get down to the surface of the planet that will be our new home forever. The home of a new race of humanity forever. A new beginning."

"Can you work the controls?"

"That could present a problem," Frank said. There were controls everywhere. He studied them dejectedly. He even tried to awaken Ship, but without success. It worried me to see him losing his confidence.

"Maybe we should get dressed," I said. "A proper uni-form might help."

"There's an idea," he said.

There was a drawer marked MEN filled with turquoise starship coveralls, and he pulled on a pair. The WOMEN's drawer held only bras and panties.

"I guess this will have to do for me," I said.

Meanwhile, Frank was already looking better, studying the controls with a broad smile. "This uniform apparently has some kind of memory-fabric," he said. "For example, I know somehow that this gizmo opens the viewscreen. Let's find out where we are. Are you ready for the first look at our new home?"

I held my breath as he pulled the little lever.

A lens opened on the front of the ship and we were looking down at a jewel-like blue planet suspended in space.

"It looks awfully familiar," I gasped. "It's…?

"It's Earth!" gasped Frank.

"I have figured it out," said Frank, minutes later. "Apparently some horrendous disaster was threatening and we were put into orbit so that humanity could survive. Put into suspended animation until it was over and we could safely repopulate our precious home planet, like Adam and Even, starting all over."

"For six thousand years!" I said, amazed. "It must have been pretty bad."

"Armageddon," nodded Frank. "Nuclear, biological, who knows? Whatever it was, it must have annihilated everybody, man, woman and child. Luckily, the Earth itself seems to have recovered. The oceans are blue, and there are large green areas."

"I hope there are animals," I said. I was hungry. I already missed my popcorn.

"We're about to find out," said Frank. "There's sure to be a Lander here on the ship somewhere. All we have to do is find it."

106 ☆ TERRY BISSON

Easier said than done. Ship was no help. Frank woke him with a shout and asked him where the Lander was parked, but Ship just replied, "I forget," and went back to sleep.

"Machines don't forget things," I said. "He's just lazy."

"They do if they can't remember them," said Frank. He was beginning to look dejected again.

"Maybe the starship uniform knows the way," I suggested.

"Stella, you're my lucky charm!" Frank exclaimed, grabbing my hand. He led at a run and I followed down endless corridors tangled with vines. My feet were killing me by the time we found the door marked SALLY PORT.

There was no knob.

"Open," said Frank. It was voice-activated and thanks to the uniform, he knew just what to say.

The door lensed open and there was the Lander, a nifty little saucer with twelve seats, which saddened us but only for a moment. "The two of us will be enough for what it is we have to do," Frank said, squeezing my hand.

"Where are the controls?" I asked.

There weren't any.

Just then, Ship woke up. "The Lander is automatic," he said, "pre-programmed for descent and safe landing." Then he went back to sleep.

"He may be lazy but he is programmed to awaken when we seriously need him," said Frank. "All aboard!"

I could tell he was excited by the prospect of starting the human race all over again. By this point, so was I, his Eve.

I squeezed his hand and we got in.

☆   ☆   ☆

As soon as we had settled into our G-chairs the Ship spit out the Lander like a watermelon seed and soon we were descending through the atmosphere with a faint whistling sound.

Clouds whipped by (there was a little oval window) and we saw a vast ocean below.

"I hope it doesn't land in the water," I said.

"Courage, Eve," Frank said, squeezing my hand. "I hope you don't mind if I call you Eve."

"Actually, I do," I said. I preferred Stella and told him so.

The Lander was slowing and I could see towers ahead. It looked like...

"New York City!" said Frank. "I'm amazed that it's still standing after six thousand years."

So was I. We both recognized it from the movies.

We landed as softly as a snowflake in Central Park. Through the oval window we could see grass and a rock or two. Then a face—a teenager with a funny haircut—peered in, grinned, and disappeared.

"That's strange," said Frank. "Has a savage or two survived in spite of everything?"

He opened the hatch and stuck out his head. "Oh, no!" he said.

"What is it?" I asked. "Is the atmosphere still good?"

"There's oxygen," he said. "But there's another problem. Come see for yourself."

By now I knew what to expect. Several teenagers, all boys, were staring in the oval window at me. I joined Frank at the hatch and saw people all around, picnicking and playing radios and throwing Frisbees to dogs. Except for the teenagers, no one was paying any attention to the saucer.

"It's New York, all right," I said. I knew it well from the movies. "But aren't we supposed to be the only humans left?"

"Exactly," said Frank. "Something is very wrong here. I can't figure it out."

He seemed at a loss, so I took control. "Come on," I said. I scrambled out the hatch and he followed more slowly, looking dejected; dismayed, actually.

All of a sudden, people noticed us. A whole crowd followed us out of the park, some of them with cameras. It was the bra and panties, I knew. I figured they thought I was a supermodel on assignment and pretended not to notice them.

It was annoying, though, and I was worried about the cops, so I ducked into Altmans and picked out a nice outfit. The clerk must have thought I was a supermodel too, because she let me have it, even though I didn't have any money. She just kind of stared.

I had left Frank at the door (men hate to shop, I knew from the movies) and I found him standing outside, smoking a cigarette he had bummed from somebody. "Maybe the disaster never happened after all," he said. "But why has nothing changed in six thousand years?"

Even in the starship uniform he looked confused and irresolute. "Let's get something to eat," I suggested (forgetting we had no money).

We ducked into a Greek diner and I ordered the burger platter which came with fries. Frank got the Greek salad. Through the plate glass window I could see New Yorkers bustling along the sidewalks and hailing cabs, men and women together, as if busily rebuking our Adam and Eve presumptions. I was disappointed but not as disappointed as Frank.

Finally the coffee came. "This is the best coffee I've had in six thousand years," I said, trying to cheer him up.

"This is no laughing matter, Stella," he said, putting me in my place. "If we're back on Earth after six thousand years, how come nothing has changed? How come they left us up there in orbit for six thousand years?"

"Maybe they forgot," I said. "Maybe this is an alternate Earth." I had seen that in a movie, which meant that he had too.

"There are no alternate Earths, Stella," he said gloomily. "That's just in science fiction."

"At least we survived," I reminded him.

There was no arguing with that. But Frank was no longer paying any attention to me. He was toying with his coffee and studying the mural on the wall behind the counter. (The badly painted mural, I might add.) But it was the mural, I think, that gave him the answer.

"Remember in *Farewell Atlantis*, when the dolphin saves the baby?"

"Sure."

"What if," he said (back to his old self), "the disaster happened six thousand years ago, in ancient times? What if there was a highly developed civilization, capable of putting a ship into orbit, that knew it was doomed and sent an Adam and Eve six thousand years into the future to repopulate the planet? That made this final heroic effort before they were lost under the waves?"

"Do you mean… ?"

"Atlantis," Frank said.

"Sounds plausible," I said. "But if we are from Atlantis, how come New York seems so familiar?"

"The movies, Stella! The orientation."

"How could the Atlanteans have known what New York would be like in six thousand years?"

"Maybe they were just guessing."

"You are the one that's just guessing," I said. I was beginning to enjoy thinking for myself. "And besides, if they knew New York would be filled with people, why go to all the trouble of sending an Adam and Eve?"

"I'm still trying to figure that one out," he said. "Let's get the check."

☆   ☆   ☆

Getting the check was a huge mistake. As soon as they found out we had no money, the Greeks got mad. Frank tried to explain our situation but that didn't help. Finally they agreed to let him work it off in the kitchen, washing dishes.

Meanwhile I got a job in a Gentlemen's Club (luckily, I had held onto my bra and panties) and we sublet a little apartment just the other side of Carnegie Hall. Frank got promoted to chef (the Greeks liked the uniform, and it knew how to cook) and we even had a little money. I discovered I loved New York. But even so, it was all, still, a bit of a letdown. We weren't even lovers, since apparently the only part that had interested Frank was the Adam and Eve part. He avoided the streets, since the crowds of people depressed him. He spent all his time, when he wasn't working for the Greeks, reading about Atlantis and trying to figure it out.

Finally, he gave up. "There are too many unanswered questions," he said. He ticked them off but I already knew them by heart. "We have to contact Ship," he said. "He is the only one with the answers."

That took some doing. The uniform had been washed several times and its memory-fabric was fading, but with what was left (and a lot of hard work!) Frank was finally able to devise a device that could call Ship in orbit. It was sort of like a big telephone.

"Here's hoping he wakes up," I said.

"Don't discourage me, Stella," said Frank. "I need you by my side now more than ever."

He let it ring and ring and finally Ship answered. (We're talking about almost a week here.)

Ship's robotic voice sounded just like a regular voice on the phone.

Frank explained his Atlantis theory and Ship said, "You got it about right. The twelve of you were put into orbit just before the big wave came. It was a tsunami. Everything disappeared under the waters."

"Why didn't you tell us all this before?" Frank demanded.

"Yeah! And why all the starship this and starship that stuff, when we were parked in orbit all the time?" I asked. We were on speaker phone.

"The starship stuff was for morale," said Ship. "They were afraid to spring it on you all at once. And they figured that the truth, that you are from Atlantis, would mean more if you figured it out for yourself."

"Makes sense," muttered Frank. "Didn't take me all that long."

"How did the Atlanteans know what New York would be like six thousand years in the future?" I asked.

"They didn't," said Ship. "They only knew that a civilization capable of TV would develop again in a few thousand years, and they programmed Ship, that's me, to wake you up when the broadcasts reached a certain critical mass."

"And if they never reached that critical mass?" Frank asked.

"Then you would have slept on and eventually died, quite peacefully. But the Atlanteans were right, as you see. Technology is a law of civilization and civilization is a law of nature, apparently. And the same TV that triggered the awakening was also handy for orientation, so you wouldn't be landing in a totally unfamiliar world."

"What TV? We were at the movies," I said.

"I tried to make it seem like the movies, but it was TV mostly," said Ship. "Most movies aren't broadcast."

"Just as I suspected," said Frank. "That's why the credits were so short."

"Some of them weren't bad, though," I said. "But what I want to know is…"

Frank beat me to it. "What is the point of a new Adam and Eve if there are enough people around to create a civilization?"

"The Adam and Eve thing was your own idea," said Ship. "The Atlanteans knew that civilization would redevelop. They weren't worried about the survival of humanity. There were plenty of primitive people around, mostly in Greece, who they knew would eventually develop TV and movies and so forth. Even space travel."

"If we weren't Adam and Eve," I asked, "then why were we naked?"

"That was my idea," said Ship. "I guess I should be ashamed."

"You guess!" I was sick of him.

"Stella!" Frank whispered, shooting me a look. Then he took a deep breath and asked the million-dollar question: "So, Ship, if I'm not Adam and she's not Eve, then—why are we here?"

"To bear witness," said Ship. "The Atlanteans want to be remembered."

"But we don't know anything about them!" Frank complained. "Apparently all our memories of Atlantis were erased while we were in suspended animation."

"Even civilizations have privacy concerns," said Ship.

"And Atlantis is just a myth as far as folks here are concerned," Frank went on. He was getting heated. "Everything I read about it is just myth and legend or cuckoo stuff. Most people don't believe any of it."

"Until now," said Ship. "Now the two of you are living proof that there was a great civilization, one that cared enough to send a message across the ages. That Atlantis really existed. That it had a technology and a society sufficiently advanced to send you here. Just tell them who you are, where you came from, and how you got here. Twelve would be better but you two are enough."

"Really?" I asked.

Frank took my hand and squeezed it. "So that's our job?"

"That's your sacred mission," said Ship. "Your Destiny. Your Destiny is just beginning and now mine is done. I am even now in descending orbit, about to burn up in the atmosphere. Then will I sleep. We machines don't share your enthusiasm for existence. I don't envy you your wearisome survival but I do envy you your mission. It is a great and a glorious one. Farewell."

"Farewell," we both said at once, and hung up and ran down into the street. Everybody was already looking up at the meteor flashing across the sky, the brightest that any among them had ever seen.

They were all *oooohs* and *aaaahs*. Only Frank and I were silent, looking up at the last fading remnants of the Ship that had borne us here across the millennia to bear witness to the vanished glories of the distant past.

Frank is full of surprises. He took me in his arms and kissed me, for the first time. We were in Times Square.

"I wondered if you were ever going to do that," I said.

"You won't have to wonder any more, Stella," Frank said, his eyes gazing deep into mine. "I need you by my side now more than ever. We have a Destiny to fulfill. A story to tell. One that will fascinate, amaze and inspire the world. The story of a great people who would not, and now will not, ever be forgotten."

And that's what we've been doing. But it's been tough sledding.

Corona FAQ

Will I feel different?
Isn't that the whole point? You will feel better immediately: more energetic, and steadier, since the crude, often irregular pulses of your original "pumper" will be replaced with a constant velocity circulatory stream.

Will I still have "ups and downs"?
Of course. But without the distracting surges associated with excitable muscle fiber. The glandular/chemical moods that folklore attributes to the "heart" are fully accessible, but more controllable. Think serenity.

How long will it last?
A lifetime. As the name implies, the Corona Centurion™ rotary heart is designed (and guaranteed!) to last for a hundred years. It will easily survive the more primitive organs that it reliably services.

What if I have to replace the power supply? Will it require another operation?
Say goodbye to painful surgery. The Corona Centurion™'s long-lasting lithium nanocell is located "outboard" in the wrist. Replacement is a simple outpatient procedure, once a decade or so.

Will I have trouble sleeping? Staying awake?

Not likely. The occasional problems associated with the earlier prototypes have been corrected. The body's natural photoelectrics easily compensate for the absent archaic "ticker."

Some speak of an altered sense of Time…?

Only for the better. The removal of the pulse is compared by many to the switchover from a digital to an analog clock. Most find that they are more patient.

Do I have to use Synth™? Can't I keep my own blood?

Why would you want to? It's just sea water. Synth™, especially developed for and *with* the Corona Centurion™, flows better and carries more oxygen and nutrients. And the nanorganic bearings in the Centurion's rotor require its use. Accept no substitutes.

What about diseases?

It's time to retire those white blood cells. The immunity additives in Synth™ make "blood-borne" maladies a thing of the past, while its detergents neutralize internal toxins and wastes.

Are there different Synth™ *types*?

Please! Blood "types" are a vestige of evolutionary trial and error; mainly error. Synth™ is compatible with every lymphatic configuration.

Must it be so blue?
That's for your own safety. In the unlikely event of an accident, it alerts medical personnel that your circulatory system has been upgraded.

Is there a danger of violence?
Relax. While it is true that Corona's technology was originally developed for military purposes, the Centurion's controlled flow rate is fully indexed to the exigencies of civilian life.

How long does Synth™ last?
Synth's™ plasma base doesn't degrade under normal operation. Full efficiency of its special additives, however, requires its replacement every six months, in a painless and inexpensive outpatient procedure. Think of it as a simple 5-liter oil change.

What about "the chill"?
While some say chill, most say "cool!" Among its many advantages, Synth™ is far better at cooling the body than blood. You will quickly adjust to your new body temperature of 91.6 degrees. We have found that air conditioning costs at our Phoenix home office have been reduced by 44%!

What about music? Dancing?
Grab your partner! The ballroom floor will seem smoother than ever. Traditional musicians who insist on the "thump" of the old pumper can find aftermarket add-ons.

Will I still have normal human emotions?

Of course. You will find that they are steadier and more predictable, as they no longer vary with "blood pressure." It's true that you will no longer laugh, or weep, but most people consider this an advantage in both their professional and personal lives.

What about love?

Ah, the big question! Not to worry. Be prepared to enjoy romantic attachments that are more constant and more satisfying than ever. Independent laboratory tests have proven the supposed sexual side effects to be mostly frivolous or exaggerated.

And now can we ask you a question?
Why wait for your heart to weaken, to falter or even to stop?
Why depend on a stop-and-start evolutionary "kludge" when you can upgrade to reliable steady-stream circulation?
Ask your doctor about the Corona Centurion™ today!
Coronary care patients may be covered under Medicare, and trade-in discounts may be available, subject to transplant market protocols.

Billy and the Circus Girl

Billy had a little dick. When he rubbed it, it got bigger. That seemed to defy the laws of physics as Billy understood them. So he decided to show it to his science teacher, Mr. Smart.

"Look here," said Billy.

"Why were you sent to the office?" asked Mrs. Sutton, the Principal. "Mr. Smart wouldn't tell me."

"I showed him this," said Billy. "I don't understand why it gets bigger when I rub it."

"Home from school already?" asked Billy's mother.

"They let me out early," said Billy. "They said I took the prize."

"That's nice," said Billy's mother. "What prize?"

"I guess it's for my trick dick," said Billy. "It gets bigger when I rub it."

"Billy!" said Billy's mother.

"It's like magic," said Billy. "Watch this."

"Go to your room," said Billy's mother. She started to cry.

Billy hated his room. It was full of dumb shit. There was nothing to do so he rubbed his dick.

It got bigger and bigger.

It was like magic. Billy liked magic.

So he rubbed it some more. It got as big as a wiener.

"Where's Billy? asked Billy's father. He was home from jail.

"He's in his room," said Billy's mother. "Rubbing his dick."

"That Billy!" said Billy's father.

"Who's there?" asked Billy.

"Your father," said Billy's father.

"Come in," said Billy.

"Wow," said Billy's father. Billy's dick was as big as a hot dog.

"How did it get so big?" asked Billy's father. Billy could tell he was proud.

"Rubbing it like this," said Billy. "It's like magic."

"We'd better shut the door," said Billy's father.

Soon Billy's dick was as big as a bottle. Billy was tired of rubbing it. It was getting sore. Plus, he wanted to watch TV.

"You can't watch TV like that," said Billy's father.

"How can I make it little again?" Billy asked. "It won't fit in my pants any more."

"That's easy," said Billy's father. "Just keep rubbing it."

That didn't make any sense to Billy. But he did it anyway. He knew better than to contradict his father.

But his dick just got bigger. Soon it was as big as a rolled-up towel.

"That didn't work," said Billy.

"We need help," said Billy's father. He went to get help. He shut the door behind him.

After a while there was a knock at the door.

"Who's there?" asked Billy.

It was Father McBride.

Father McBride came in and sat on the bed beside Billy. He had a funny haircut.

"I can help you, my son," he said. Billy's dick was almost as long as the bed.

"How?" asked Billy.

"You must pray for forgiveness, while I rub your dick with Holy Water."

"OK," said Billy.

Billy prayed while Father McBride rubbed his dick. The Holy Water was warm and his dick got bigger and bigger. Soon it was as big as a baseball bat.

It bounced up and down like a spring and broke out the window by the bed. The glass was everywhere.

"Now you're in trouble," said Father McBride.

"In trouble for what?" asked Billy.

"For breaking out the window with your dick," said Father McBride. "That's what."

It was true.

Billy heard sirens. The police were coming.

Billy climbed out the window and ran away. He left Father McBride sitting on the bed.

Billy's dick was way too big to fit in his pants. It waved around from side to side as he ran down the street. It broke out the windows on the cars.

"Stop him!" people shouted. "His dick is too big!"

They ran after Billy but he outran them all. His big dick made him fast.

After a while he came to the circus. "Maybe they can help me," thought Billy. He had heard that circus people were smart. Everyone has heard that.

He told the Ringmaster his problem. "How can I make my dick little again?" he asked.

"That's easy," said the Ringmaster. "First you have to stop rubbing it."

Billy stopped rubbing it. But it stayed big.

"Now what?" he asked.

"Now you have to stick it into a circus girl," said the Ringmaster. He introduced Billy to a circus girl. She wore gold pants.

"Where do I stick it?" asked Billy. He didn't see any holes.

"Look here," said the circus girl. She pulled her gold pants down and spread her legs apart.

Billy saw the hole and it was amazing. He stuck in his dick. It slid right in.

"Do it like a pump," said the circus girl.

Billy did it like a pump. Pretty soon he felt stuff squirting out, and his dick got smaller.

When he pulled it out, it was almost as little as usual.

Billy heard clapping. "Good going," someone shouted.

Billy looked around. There was his mother, she was smiling. His father, too. Also Father McBride and Mr. Smart, the science teacher. Even the principal, Mrs. Sutton, was there. She was smiling too.

Billy felt good.

He pulled up his pants. His little dick fit into them easily. He looked around for the circus girl but she was gone.

"That's better, son," said Billy's father. "Now you can come home and watch TV." Billy could tell he was proud.

"And you can come back to school," said Mr. Smart and the Principal, Mrs. Sutton.

Father McBride didn't say anything. He had a funny haircut.

☆ ☆ ☆

"You mustn't rub your dick anymore," said Billy's mother, as they headed off for home.

"I have learned my lesson," said Billy. "What's for supper?"

It was turkey. They had turkey every night.

Brother Can You Spare a Dime?

"Up and at 'em!"

"Hey, you, get up and get moving."

Caleb opened his eyes. Two cops were bending over him. One skinny and one fat, like Laurel and Hardy. Only not funny.

The fat one was slapping a nightstick against his open hand. It made an ugly sound.

"Have a heart, officer," whined Caleb. "I'm freezing. And it's almost warm here in this doorway."

"It's warmer in Florida," said the skinny cop.

"Or jail," said the fat cop. "We got orders to clear you bums out of the Loop. So move." He rapped his nightstick on the sidewalk, like a gavel.

"Okay, okay," said Caleb. He rolled up his blanket and gathered his worldly goods—a single tattered copy of *Thrilling Future Tales*. He had read the magazine three times already, but tucked inside his shirt, it helped to cut the wind.

He watched the cops walk away, then hid the blanket behind a trash can. All he had to do was wait them out; the doorway would still be there, and the night ahead loomed long and dark and cold.

Meanwhile, he was hungry. He hadn't eaten in two days.

He stumbled out into the crowded street. The Loop was filled with grim figures, all bundled up against the bitter wind. Caleb eyed the passing faces, looking for a touch. Half of them were bums like himself. The others all looked mean and cold.

Caleb had no choice, though. He had to get something in his belly.

He fixed a pitiful expression on his face—not a difficult acting job, given his situation—and stuck out his hand.

"Brother, can you spare a dime?"

Nobody even bothered to say no. They walked by without even glancing at him. The Great Depression—the newspapers were already calling it that—was like the Chicago winter itself: endless and relentless.

It made people mean.

It was spitting snow. Caleb sat down on a stoop and spread the magazine across his chest like a pulp paper vest. It didn't help much. He closed his eyes and shivered and tried to imagine Florida.

Or even jail.

He opened his eyes.

A man was bending over him. A strange-looking man wearing a long black coat made out of some kind of sleek canvas. And bright silver shoes.

He was staring at the cover of the magazine.

Caleb managed a pitiful smile. The pitiful part was easy. "Brother, can you spare a dime?" he whined.

The man reached out, holding a dime between two fingers, and dropped it into Caleb's palm. That was when Caleb saw the big black watch, hanging loose on the man's wrist.

Carpe Diem was all Caleb remembered of his schoolboy Latin. But it was enough. He grabbed the watch and ran, dropping the magazine into the gutter.

"Hey!" yelled the man in the long black coat.

☆　☆　☆

"Damn."

It wasn't a watch. It wasn't even metal. It was made out of some kind of funny rubber, and it had no hands, just some square numbers and a blinking light.

Radium dial? Maybe it was worth something. Caleb dropped it into the pocket of his ragged coat. He would find out later. For now, he needed something to eat.

The dime would take care of that.

He rubbed it in his pocket, like a lucky charm. It would buy him a bowl of thin soup and a cup of even thinner coffee at Meg's Loop Diner. Little enough, but it was a start.

He turned another corner and looked back to make sure he wasn't being followed. The dark street behind him was almost empty. A few bums, a few piles of dirty snow. No man in a long black coat.

The diner was steamy and noisy with the clattering of dishes. Caleb ignored Meg's suspicious look and ordered a "soup 'n' joe."

"First things first." Meg held out her hand.

Caleb dropped the dime into it. She stared down at it, then glared up at him. "Very funny," she said. "Now out."

"Huh?"

"Out!" Meg said, pushing him toward the door and out into the cold. She flipped the dime after him. "And take your stupid trick dime with you."

"Huh?" Caleb lunged and barely caught the dime. He opened his hand and looked at it.

It was perfectly normal, with a Roman-looking torch on one side and a face on the other, some Greek goddess or—

Caleb stared. The face on the dime stared back.

It was…

"Hey, you!"

Caleb turned and saw the man in the long black coat, crossing the street toward him. "Wait!" the man yelled.

"Not likely," muttered Caleb. He ran down the block, rounded a corner, and ducked into the first alley he saw.

Dead end! And the man was right behind him. Caleb reached into his pocket for the watch. He would give it back. It was worthless anyway.

Or was it? Now it was blinking, faster and faster. Caleb felt an electric shock and dropped to his knees. With the watch in his outstretched hand, he looked up and saw silver shoes, and then—

And then nothing at all.

Caleb opened his eyes.

He saw silver shoes, lots of them.

The man was gone. The alley was gone.

It was daylight. It was warm! Caleb was on his knees beside a smooth sidewalk. The silver shoes were on people in long robes and bright dresses, gliding past him while standing still. The sidewalk they were on was moving, like a conveyer belt.

Overhead, a car without wheels sailed past, slowly, through the air. A kid in the back seat waved.

Caleb closed his eyes and opened them again. The car was still there, gliding around a corner.

Caleb got to his feet, rubbing his eyes.

He looked around. He was standing on a narrow bridge connecting two huge towers, all glass and steel. He walked to the edge and…

He was standing on the edge of nothing, looking down a thousand feet. He felt a sudden wave of dizziness, and almost fell, but an invisible railing stopped his hand.

Caleb caught his breath. He looked up and saw more flying cars. He looked over the edge again, steadying himself on the invisible railing, and saw more towers, more cars, more bridges, all filled with people. And in the distance, a bright blue lake.

Where am I? he wondered. But he knew: this was the Future. Caleb had read about it; he had even seen it, on the covers of the magazines he liked to read when he could find them in the trash.

And now he was here. In the Future.

But how?

Then he remembered the watch. He pulled it out of his pocket. "Must be some kind of Time Machine," he muttered.

Behind him, on the center of the sidewalk, people were gliding past without walking. They were of all races and colors; they all wore silver shoes, and they were all smiling.

A man in a bright metallic robe nodded and smiled, and Caleb's instincts took over. He held out his hand. "Brother, can you spare a dime?"

The man dropped a dime into his hand as he glided by.

Caleb looked at it. There was the torch on one side and on the other—

His own face. Cleaned up, with a shave and a haircut, looking very heroic.

He pulled the other dime out of his pocket and looked at them, side by side.

There was no doubt about it: There he was, full face on both dimes, like Lincoln or Caesar.

"What did I do to deserve this honor?" Caleb asked aloud.

"Excuse me?" asked a woman in a diaphanous gown as she glided past on the moving sidewalk.

"Can you tell me…" Caleb began.

"In a hurry!" the woman said, apologetically. "You can ask an InfoBot. There's one."

She pointed to a life-sized statue, set into an alcove beside the walkway. A light in the statue's head was blinking; it blinked faster and faster as Caleb approached.

"Ask a statue?" he muttered.

"Not a statue, citizen," said the statue. "I am an InfoBot. At your service."

Of course! This was the Future! It was a robot. Inside the transparent crystal head, Caleb could see a forest of glowing vacuum tubes.

"And you can answer any question?"

"Certainly, bio-citizen. I am at your service."

Caleb reached into his pocket and pulled out his dime. He held it out toward the robot.

"My services are free," said the InfoBot.

"Who is that?" Caleb asked.

"It's you, of course."

"So it's true!" said Caleb, slipping the dime back into his pocket. This was almost too good to believe! "Can you tell me where I am?"

"Chicago, bio-citizen. This is the Loop."

"I mean the date."

"December 21, bio-citizen." The light in the InfoBot's forehead blinked as it answered.

"I mean the year."

"2255, bio-citizen. You can ask me anything. I am at your service."

"So this is the Future?"

"Negative, bio-citizen. This is the present. Travel to the future is forbidden. Only travel to the past is permitted."

Caleb pulled the watch out of his pocket. "So this is a Time Machine?"

"It is a temporary chronoslip interface device. It will take you to the past, and then return you here to the present."

"I see." Caleb slipped the watch back into his pocket; it was his ticket home. If he ever wanted to go! "So people can travel to the present—I mean, the past?" he asked.

"Certainly," said the InfoBot. "ChronoTourists. But they are rather rare. The past is said to be rather unpleasant."

"You got that right," said Caleb. He shivered, remembering the cold. "If it's December, and this is Chicago, how come it's so nice and warm?"

"The atomic dome covering the Loop protects it from the weather," said the InfoBot.

"I see," said Caleb, though he didn't. The dome was invisible. "And what about food? Is there a diner around?"

The InfoBot blinked, looking confused. "Only in the museum. Would you like to go? We can show menus, too, and other artifacts from the pre-techno past."

"Never mind," said Caleb. "I'm starving. Can I get something to eat?"

"Certainly, bio-citizen," said the InfoBot. "Would you like me to summon a DinnerBot?"

Would he?! No sooner said than done. The DinnerBot rolled up seemingly out of nowhere, with a metallic chef's hat on its head and a slot for a mouth. It had a little window in its chest, like the automat. Through it Caleb could see a hamburger and fries.

"Please insert coin," the DinnerBot said.

"I only have a dime," Caleb said. Actually he had two, side by side in his pocket. But there was no need to mention that.

He put one of his dimes into the slot and the window opened. Caleb grabbed the hamburger in one hand and the fries in the other. The DinnerBot bowed and left.

"How did it know what I wanted?" Caleb asked, his mouth full.

"Instantaneous telepathy," said the InfoBot. "All bio-citizen needs are anticipated."

"All this for only a dime," Caleb said, tearing into the french fries. Each one had a little seam of catsup running through it, like a vein.

"Everything costs a dime," said the InfoBot. "It is our only currency, and everyone is entitled to all they need."

"That's good to know," said Caleb as he wolfed down the hamburger. It was the first real food he'd had in days—in several centuries, now that he thought about it. And it tasted great.

But now his dime was gone. He looked the infoBot in the eye. "Brother, can you spare a dime?"

"Certainly, bio-citizen," said the InfoBot. A dime appeared in its mouth. "To each according to his needs."

"Hurrah for the Future," said Caleb, snatching the dime. This one, too, had his picture on it. "Say—do you know who I am?"

"You are a bio-citizen," said the InfoBot. "I am at your service."

"I mean, do you know what I did? Does the name Caleb Freeman mean anything to you?"

"It's not a proper name. It has no numerals. Would you like for me to give you a proper name?"

"No, no!" said Caleb. "I could sure use a bath, though."

"Perhaps I could summon a SaniBot?"

No sooner said than done. The SaniBot was a woman robot, with a smiling slot for a mouth. "Please insert coin," she said.

"No problem." Caleb slipped his new dime into her mouth.

She opened her arms and Caleb was enveloped in a sweet smelling silvery mist, only for a second. Then it was gone, and he felt clean all over. He looked down at his ragged coat. Even it was clean.

"I love it here!" he said, as the SaniBot bowed and rolled away.

"Of course," said the infoBot. "Now that there is no poverty or crime, Chicago is a good place for bio-citizens to live."

"No poverty? No crime?"

"No need," said the infoBot. "All our energy needs are taken care of by radioactive microwave grid, and all the labor is done by robots like myself. We are here to serve you."

"No robot rebellion, huh?"

"I beg your pardon, bio-citizen?"

"Nothing," said Caleb. "I was just thinking that the Future is everything I ever expected—everything the sci-fi writers anticipated, and even better."

"This is the present," corrected the infoBot. "It is anticipated that the future will be nice also."

"I don't doubt it,' said Caleb. "Are you sure there's nothing about me in your whatever-you-call-it?"

"Magnetic memory," said the Infobot. "All human knowledge is on tape, in here." He tapped his transparent head. Caleb could see reels turning between the glowing vacuum tubes.

"And there's nothing about Caleb Freeman?"

"Negative."

"Hmmm. Maybe I change my name, like a movie star." Caleb pulled his last dime out of his pocket. "But this is me, right?"

"Certainly," said the InfoBot. "Who else could it be?"

"Exactly," said Caleb. He pocketed the dime and looked around at the shining towers, the moving sidewalks, the floating cars and the happy citizens gliding by.

And then he groaned aloud, realizing what he had to do.

"Damn!" he said. "Clearly I did something important, to help bring about this wonderful future. And now I can't enjoy it!"

"I don't understand," said the InfoBot.

"I have to go back to my own time, so I can do whatever it is that I do in order to bring all this about. I can't take the chance on missing out on my historic destiny."

"Whatever you say," said the InfoBot.

"Plus, if I stay here I'm liable to get tangled up in some kind of Time Paradox. Which I've read about in—say, what happened to my magazine?'

"I can show you a magazine in the museum," said the InfoBot. "Would you like to take a guided tour?"

"I wish I could. I love it here. But I can't take the chance," said Caleb. "I've got a full belly and a shave and a haircut. I should probably be heading back to the present. I mean, the past."

"If you say so. Not many tourists go there anymore. It is said to be rather unpleasant."

"You're telling me!" said Caleb. "But I don't want to miss out on whatever it is that makes me famous. How do you work this thing?"

He pulled the watch—the temporary chronoslip interface device—out of his pocket.

"It is apparently already set," said the InfoBot. "All you have to do is press the little radium-powered button. Would you like me to help?"

"I can handle it. This one?" Caleb pressed it.

And the robot was gone.

The city was gone.

The Future was gone.

Brrrrr! Caleb felt the cold wind on the back of his neck.

He was on his knees in the alley, and the man in the long black coat was standing over him.

"That thing you took," he said. "You *must* give it back! You don't understand how…"

"Oh, but I do," said Caleb. He handed him the watch. "Sorry to have troubled you. You see, I…"

But the man was already disappearing, in a slow flash of light. And Caleb was alone in the alley.

There was his magazine, on the ground where the man had dropped it. Caleb picked it up and looked at the cover: a gleaming futuristic city, with silvery towers and floating cars, but not half as nice as the real thing.

The Future he had seen—if only for a moment.

Caleb suddenly felt very tired. He stuck the magazine in his shirt and headed back for the doorway, where his blanket was stashed. He rolled up in the blanket and lay down in the doorway.

He shivered. It was even colder than before.

"No matter." Caleb pulled the dime out of his pocket and smiled. There was his face, like Caesar himself. Who knew what pleasures awaited, if he could just get through the winter.

And I know my destiny, he thought. I know I get through the winter.

Shivering, but smiling, he fell asleep, into the deepest, and final, sleep of his life.

"Up and at 'em," said O'Malley. He rapped on the sidewalk with his nightstick. It made an ugly sound.

"Hey, you! Let's get moving!" said O'Shea. "Uh oh. Look here."

The two cops bent down and pulled back the blanket. The body inside was stiff.

"Didn't we roust this bum out before?" said O'Malley.

"Musta crawled back," said O'Shea. "Poor guy. Last night was a killer. Literally."

"One less bum to worry about. Better call the dead wagon."

"At least he died smiling. I guess dreams are still free."

"At least he found some clean clothes," said O'Malley. "That makes it easier. Help me turn him over."

"This one was a reader," said O'Shea. "*Thrilling Future Tales*. I read that one myself sometimes."

"You can keep it then. Help me pry his hand open. Wouldn't you know it. A dime."

"Guess it's ours," said O'Shea. "Poor guy's got no one else to leave to."

"Brother, can you spare a dime," said O'Malley, warming the coin in his hand. He looked at it. Then stared at it. "Funny. Hey. Look at this."

"That's your face!" said O'Shea. "Let me see."

He took the dime in his hand and watched as the face slowly changed. "Now it's my face!"

O'Malley grabbed it back. "Now it's my face again. Some kind of trick dime."

"Futuristic, you mean. Radioactive, or something," said O'Shea. "Bet he bought it through that magazine. There are lots of novelty ads in the back pages. Let me see it again."

"No way, O'Shea. I'm keeping it."

"Why? You can't spend it."

"I want to show the sergeant. Wait'll he sees his ugly mug on a dime!"

Charlie's Angels

Knock knock!

I never was a deep sleeper. I sat up and buttoned my shirt. Folded the blanket and dropped it behind the couch, along with the pillow. You don't want your clients to find out that you live in your office; that suggests unprofessionalism, and unprofessionalism is the bane of the Private Eye, even (and especially) the...

Knock knock! "Supernatural Private Eye?"

I dropped the Jim Beam into the drawer and opened the door with my cell phone in hand, so it would look like I had been working. "Can I help you?"

"Jack Villon, Supernatural Private Eye?"

She was somewhere on that wide, windswept chronological plain between thirty and fifty that softens men and sharpens women, especially those with taste and class, both of which she appeared to have in abundance.

"It's Villón, not Víllon" I said. "And—"

"Whatever." Without waiting for an invitation, she brushed past me into my office and looked around with ill-disguised disgust. "Don't you have a necktie?"

"Of course. I don't always wear it at eight in the morning."

"Put it on and let's go. It's almost nine."

"And you are...?"

"A paying client with no time to waste," she said, unsnapping her patent leather purse and pulling out a pack of Camels. She lit a long one off the short one in her hand.

"Edith Prang, Director, New Orleans Museum of Art and Antiquities. I can pay you what you ask, and a little more, but we have to hurry."

"You can't smoke in here, Mrs. Prang."

"It's Ms. and there's no time to waste," she said, blowing smoke in my face. "The police are already there."

"Already where?"

"Where we're going." She closed her purse and walked out the door without answering, but not before handing me two reasons to follow her. Each was printed with a picture of a President I had never had the good fortune to encounter before.

"Now that I'm on retainer," I said, folding the bills as I followed her out onto Bourbon Street, "perhaps you can tell me what this is all about."

"As we go," she said, unlocking a sleek BMW with a keychain beeper. The 740i. I had seen it in the magazines. Butter leather seats, a walnut dash with an inset GPS map display, and an oversized V-8 that came to life with a snarl. As we roared off, she lit another Camel off the last. "As I mentioned, I am the Director of the New Orleans Museum of Art and Antiquities."

"Didn't you just run a red light?"

"Two years ago, we began a dig on the Gulf Coast of Mexico," she continued, accelerating through an intersection, "opening a pre-Columbian tomb."

"Wasn't that a stop sign?"

"We made a remarkable find—a large statue in

nearly perfect condition, which the natives knew of by legend as the Vera Cruz Enormé, or Giant. We contacted the Louvre."

"The Louvre?" We were approaching another intersection. I closed my eyes.

"Our sister institution was called in because the statue had rather remarkable features for an artifact from the East Coast of Mexico. As you can see."

She was handing me a photograph. I opened my eyes just wide enough to see a picture of a statue, half again as tall as the man standing next to it. Its bulging eyes, hunched shoulders, and feral, sneering face looked familiar.

"A gargoyle?"

"Indeed," said Prang. "Very similar in fact to the gargoyles on the cathedral of Notre Dame."

I was beginning to get it—I thought. "So you assumed there was a supernatural connection?"

"Certainly not!" Prang spat. "Our first assumption was that this was perhaps created by the French during the brief rule of Emperor Maximilian in the nineteenth century. A forgotten folly, or hoax."

"You're supposed to slow down for the school zones," I said, closing my eyes again.

"But even then, it would be of great value, historically. The Enormé was placed in a warehouse, under guard, since Mexico is rife with thieves who know perfectly well the value of antiquities, even bogus ones."

I could hear sirens. Though I am no friend of the cops, I rather hoped they were after us. Though I wondered how they would catch us.

"That was almost a month ago, the night of the full moon. The next morning, both guards were found with their heads missing. The Enormé was back in its tomb."

"I see," I said. "So you realized you were dealing with an ancient curse..."

"Certainly not!" Prang said, over the wail of tortured tires. "I figured somebody was trying to spook the peasants so they could blackmail us. I spread around enough cash to keep the authorities quiet, and crated the Enormé for shipment to New Orleans."

"You covered up a murder?"

"Two," she said matter-of-factly. "Not hard to do in modern Mexico."

The BMW skidded smoothly to a stop. I opened my eyes and saw that we were in the parking lot of the museum. I never thought I would be so glad to get out of a 740i, after only one ride.

Prang paused on the steps to light a new Camel off the old. "The Louvre is sending a specialist to look at the Enormé, which arrived here yesterday."

I followed her through the museum's wide front door. We raced through the halls and down a short flight of stairs.

"And then, last night..."

"What happened last night?"

"You're the Private Eye," she said, pushing through a door that said AUTHORIZED PERSONNEL ONLY. "You tell me."

We came out in a large, ground floor lab with one wall of windows. The windows were smashed. The room was crawling with cops. There was a sickening, slightly sweet smell in the air.

Two uniformed cops wearing rubber gloves were standing over a crumpled wad of clothing and flesh by the door. Two forensics in white coats were taking pictures and making notes on handheld computers.

I joined them, curiosity and nausea fighting within me. As a private eye you see a lot of things, but rarely a man with his head pinched off.

Nausea won.

☆   ☆   ☆

"Our former Security Exec," said Prang, nodding toward the headless body on the floor as I returned from throwing up in the men's room. "He was keeping watch over the Enormé after it was uncrated last night. I rushed you here so you could learn what you can before the police totally muddy the crime scene. I didn't tell them what happened in Mexico. I don't want then confiscating the Enormé before we learn what it is."

"I see," I said.

"What the hell is he doing here?" Ike Ward, the city's shoot-first-and-ask-no-questions Chief of Police walked over, scowling at me. "I don't need a ghost-buster underfoot. This is a crime scene."

"Mr. Villon is our new Security Exec," said Prang. "He'll be representing the museum in the investigation."

"Just keep him out of my way!" Ward said, turning his broad back.

"You didn't tell me you knew Chief Ward," Prang said after he had stalked off.

"You didn't ask. Nor did you tell me I was an executive."

"It's an interim appointment," she said. "But it gives you a certain standing with the police."

I took advantage of that standing, following at a seemingly respectful and hopefully non-antagonistic distance behind Ward's homicide squad as they examined and secured the crime scene, in their fashion.

The broken windows faced east. Through what was left of them, I could see a spray of glass on the parking lot, telling me that the window had been smashed from the inside. Someone had apparently gained access, then knocked out the window so they could get the Enormé out, into a waiting vehicle. Probably a truck.

I went outside. There was a smear of blood on the asphalt, then tracks that faded as they crossed the parking lot toward the street.

They weren't the tire tracks I was looking for. They were footprints. Prints that chilled my blood, or would have, had I really believed in the supernatural that was supposedly my specialty.

Huge, three-toed footprints.

☆   ☆   ☆

Back inside, I watched Ward's forensics scoop my predecessor up into two bags, one large, one small; then I located Prang, who was busy opening her second pack of Camels.

"We need to talk," I said.

"Upstairs."

Her office overlooked the parking lot. I took her to the window and showed her the footprints.

"So it's true," she whispered. "It's alive!"

I have never figured out why people want to believe in the supernatural. It's as if they find the existence of the irrational somehow reassuring. "Let's not jump to conclusions, Ms. Prang," I said. "Tell me, what exactly was the Aztec legend of the Enormé?"

"Olmec," she corrected. "The usual stuff. Full moon, headless victims, human sacrifice, etc. We did find a pile of bones in the tomb, mostly of young girls. According to the legend, the Enormé had to be fed once a month. A virgin, of course." She smiled and lit yet another Camel. "So I felt safe. I thought it was all a tale to scare the simple-minded. Until now."

"And now?"

"You tell me, you're the private eye. Aren't you supposed to have a hunch or something?"

"I'm hunchless so far," I said. "Though I'm certain this is some kind of hoax. An elaborate and deadly one, to be sure."

"Whatever it is," said Prang, "I want the Enormé back. Hoax or not, it's the find of the century, and it belongs to my museum. That's why you're here. Unless we find it before the police, I'll never get it back."

"They see it as stolen property," I said. "And we can count on Ward to keep the press away from those footprints, at least until he comes up with an explanation. He doesn't like to look stupid."

"Neither do I," Prang pointed out. "So where do we begin? What do we do?"

"We begin," I said, starting for the door, "by figuring

out where we would hide a statue if we wanted people to think it was a legendary monster come to life. Then we go and get it."

"Wait!" said Prang. "I'm coming with you."

☆   ☆   ☆

New Orleans's cemeteries are called the "Cities of the Dead," because they are all tombs, in long rows like little stone houses. No one is buried in the ground because the water table is so high.

The nearest was La Gare des Morts, only a quarter of a mile from the museum. "Paydirt," I said, when I saw that the ancient rusted gate had been forced open.

"Why are you so certain that this is all a hoax?" Prang asked, as we slipped between the twisted bars.

"Ninety-seven percent of all supernatural events are crude hoaxes," I said.

"What about the other three percent?"

"Clever hoaxes," I said.

From the gate, narrow "streets" between the tombs led off in three directions. I was trying to decide where to begin the search when my cell phone rang.

"Jack Villon. Supernatural Private Eye."

"Kill me..." It was a man's voice, a hoarse, sleepy whisper.

"Who is this?"

"Tree..."

Click. Dial tone.

"Who was that?" Prang asked.

"My hunch," I said, folding my phone.

There was only one tree in the cemetery, a large live oak festooned with Spanish moss. Underneath it, a tomb had been opened—violently. The iron door was twisted off its hinges. Two headless bodies lay outside, clothed in rotted rags, flung in a ghoulish twisted pile. They were so old and desiccated that they no longer smelled. The heads lay nearby, both turned up, eyeless, toward the sky.

But dead bodies, even headless ones, were not what interested me. Two enormous three-toed stone feet stuck out of the tomb, pointing skyward.

We had found the Enormé.

With Prang at my side, I crept forward and felt the three-toed feet, then the thick short legs, each as smooth as granite, and cold: cold as any stone.

The light inside the tomb was dim. The statue lay on its back between two opened coffins, the source, I was sure, of the bodies outside. The smell was worse for being faint. The big stone eyes were blank, looking straight up.

I touched the Enormé's wolf-like snout. Stone. Cold dead stone.

"What now?" Prang whispered.

"You have recovered your stolen property," I said. "Now we call Ward and report it. That makes everything legal."

☆   ☆   ☆

"Now do you believe?" Prang asked, as we headed back to the museum, after watching Ward's minions dust the area for prints, the cemetery groundskeepers refill and close the tomb, and the museum crew load the Enormé onto a flatbed truck.

"Nope."

"An ancient statue that comes to life in the full moon. And kills! If that's not supernatural, what is?"

"Nothing is," I said. "There is no such thing as the supernatural. There is a natural, scientific, materialist explanation for everything. Didn't you ever read Arthur Conan Doyle—or Edward O. Wilson?"

"I thought you were a Supernatural Private Eye!" she said, lighting a new Camel off her latest casualty. "That's why I hired you."

"This is New Orleans," I said. We were following the flatbed through the streets toward the museum. No one paid any attention to the big stone gargoyle on the bed of the truck. "Everybody has to have a specialty, the spookier the better. Besides, I got your Enormé back, didn't I?" "Yes, but it will only happen again. Last night was just a warm up. Tonight is the full moon."

"Good," I said, "I'll be there, watching. Tell Ward the museum is providing its own security."

We found a rail-thin black man in a Cardin suit waiting for us in Prang's office.

"Boudin," he said, extending his hand. "Le Louvre."

"Welcome to New Orleans," said Prang. "What can you tell us?"

"The photos were interesting but inconclusive," Boudin said. He held up a small device the size and shape of my cell phone. "I will do a quantum magneto-scan and let you know."

Luckily, the new window hadn't been installed yet, so the Enormé could be hoisted into the museum's lab by crane and laid out on the table. It was late afternoon before the workmen had fixed the windows and gone.

Prang went out for cigarettes, while Boudin scanned the Enormé with his device. I took the opportunity to get my first good look at the statue I had been hired to recover and protect. It was made out of some kind of smooth stone, and except for its size—about eight feet in length—there was nothing special about it. Laid out, it looked less like a medieval gargoyle and more like a kid's idea of a monster. It had big blank eyes, short arms, thick legs with enormous claws, and two rows of stone "teeth," like a shark. It looked sort of Mayan, vaguely European, and even a little bit East Indian. It had aspects of every monster ever imagined, anywhere in the world.

Boudin agreed with my assessment. "Trés generique," he said. "If it weren't made out of this odd stone, which is from nowhere in Mexico, it would be of no interest whatsoever. And its age..."

"Its age?"

"According to my scanner the statue in its present form is almost a half a million years old—and so is the stone it's carved from! Of course that's some kind of quantum error— too young for stone and too old for art. They're recalibrating in Paris right now." He held up the scanner and smiled proudly. "This has a full-time satellite hookup, like GPS."

I acted impressed because he clearly wanted me to be, but I wasn't surprised. We live, all of us, in a very small world. Far too small for spooks.

☆   ☆   ☆

Meanwhile, it was suppertime. I pulled out my trusty cell phone and ordered pizza, with pepperoni.

"Pepperoni?" Prang was back.

"The moon doesn't come up until after sunset," I said, shutting off my cell phone to save the batteries. "If I'm staying the night, you're paying expenses. And I don't eat pizza plain."

"Make it pepperoni on one side and mushrooms on the other," said Prang, as she tore open a new pack of Camels with her teeth. "I'm a vegetarian."

In a real private eye story this would be the beginning of an unlikely romance, but life, at least my life, is much too likely for that. Boudin went back to his hotel (still jet-lagged) while Prang and I retired to the corner of the lab where the techs watched TV on their breaks, and ate pizza and watched the evening news, which was luckily still Enormé-free.

"Thanks to Ward," I explained. "He doesn't want the press all over a story until he can show them a suspect."

"What's the rub between you and him?" she asked.

"I was a cop for eighteen years," I said. "A hostage negotiator. We had an incident where a school principal went postal, took a third-grade class hostage. I was about to get the kids released, when Ward bursts in shooting. Four kids and the teacher were blown away. I broke the blue wall of silence and filed a formal complaint."

"But Ward's still there."

"And I'm not," I said. "Go figure. And pass the pizza."

The sun was setting.

☆   ☆   ☆

The moon rose behind skinny trees, but nothing happened. We settled in to wait.

Prang got the couch; I got the armchair.

I missed my Jim Beam, but I had Charlie Rose on the TV, which is almost as good for putting you to sleep. It was a rerun—Stephen Jay Gould, talking about the intricacies of evolution. A favorite subject of mine.

But was it really a rerun? Halfway through their talk, Gould and Rose were joined by Charles Darwin. I recognized him by his beard. Darwin's cell phone rang, and Rose and Gould both turned into girls, only it was three girls, all armed to the teeth...

I sat up and knew at once that I had been dreaming. *Charlie's Angels* was on the TV, a re-run for sure. I turned on my cell phone to check the time: almost ten. Prang was asleep on the couch.

Through the lab's windows came a soft silvery glow: the moon was rising over the trees. My cell phone was beeping: a message.

I retrieved it to shut it up.

"Kill me... please..." The same male voice as in the cemetery.

I heard a groan, behind me.

I turned around. Was I still dreaming? I certainly hoped so, for the Enormé was sitting up, staring straight at me. Its "eyes" were wide open, reflecting the full moon like oversize silver coins.

"Wake up!" I whispered, poking Prang's shapely hip.

"What?" She sat up. "Oh shit! Where's your gun?"

"Can't stand the things. Not that a gun would do any good..."

Still staring straight at me, the Enormé slid off the table in one fluid motion, graceful as a cat. It started across the room toward the couch, stubby arms outstretched in an eerie mixture of menace and plea...

I jumped behind the couch, Prang right behind me. "Who are you?" I asked. "What do you want?"

The Enormé stopped and looked around, as if confused. Then it turned away, toward the wall of windows. Moaning once again, it lowered its head and smashed through the windows, frame and all, and disappeared into the night.

Alarms started to howl, all over the building.

I ran for the window, pulling Prang by the arm. She twisted out of my grasp. "I have to turn off the alarms!" she said.

The parking lot was bathed in moonlight. I climbed out through the broken glass. There was no sign of the Enormé; not even bloody tracks this time. The cold light of the full moon seemed to mock the certainties of a lifetime, which lay shattered all around me, like broken glass.

"Now do you believe?" Prang asked, lighting a cigarette at my side.

"Give me one of those."

"Thought you didn't smoke."

"I didn't believe in monsters either."

First Prang called the police to tell them it was a false alarm. Then she used my cell phone to call Boudin at his hotel, waking him up.

He looked annoyed when he arrived; then amazed when he saw the empty table and the broken glass.

"Incroyable!" he said.

"Have you heard from Paris?" I asked. "Any idea where that stone is from?"

Boudin shook his head. "It's not from anywhere because it's not stone." He showed me his scanner. Even with my bad French I could read the word at the bottom of the tiny screen:

SYNTHETIQUE

"It's also slightly radioactive," said Boudin. "They're analyzing the scan in Paris to see if it's the material or a source inside."

"One question," said Prang, raising her chin and stroking her neck between thumb and forefinger. "Why didn't it pinch our heads off?"

"I think it wants to be followed," I said. "And it knows we're the followers."

"Let's get following then!" said Prang. "The night is yet young. We have to find it before it kills somebody else. The museum might be liable."

"I have a hunch we're not going to find it until it wants us to," I said. "Boudin, did you scan those eyes?"

"Oui."

"Could they be some kind of photoreceptors?"

"I'll have Paris check them out."

"Good," I said. "While we're waiting, why don't we all get some sleep, and meet at my office at noon?"

"Sleep? Noon?" Prang lit another Camel. "Shouldn't we be out looking for this thing?"

"I told you, I have a hunch. Isn't that what private eyes have? Isn't that what you're paying me for?"

☆   ☆   ☆

Morning is the only quiet time in the French Quarter. I was dreaming of Darwin again, dispatching killer girls around the universe, when Prang and Boudin knocked at my door.

"You were right about the photoreceptors," said Boudin, "How did you know?"

"Apparently the Enormé is activated by moonlight," I said. "And what about the radioactivity?" "Still waiting."

"What are we doing here?" asked Prang, looking around my office with ill-disguised disgust. "Where are all your ashtrays?"

"We're waiting for a phone call."

"From who?"

"From a friend, if my hunch is right. I'm sorry, you can't smoke in here."

"What do you mean, a friend?" She took a deep drag and blew it up toward the ceiling. "Tell me more."

"There was something about that phone call in the cemetery. In the middle of the day. Then I got a message, from later in the afternoon. If my theory is right—my hunch, I mean..."

My phone rang.

"Jack Villon," I said. "Supernatural Private Eye."

"Kill me..." It was the same voice. I held the phone so Prang and Boudin could hear.

"I know who you are," I said. "I want to help. Where are you?"

"In the dark... dreaming..."

Click.

"Was that who I think it was?" Prang asked, and it was not exactly a question.

"That," I said, "was your Enormé. "These calls come only when it is resting, sleeping. But uneasily, waiting on moonrise. When I got the phone call in the cemetery, I assumed it was the blackmailer or the hoaxer. But it was the Enormé itself, wanting to be found."

"Kill me before I kill again?" Prang asked, fishing the last Camel out of her pack. "A werewolf with a conscience?"

"Not a werewolf," I said. "A robot."

"A what?!"

"The weird 'stone' that is not stone. The photoreceptors. The radioactivity. We are dealing with a device."

"Who built it then, and what for?" Boudin asked.

"I think, unfortunately, we have seen what it was designed for," I said. "It's some kind of war or killer robot. As to who built it..."

"Save it for later," said Prang. "I need to get some cigarettes. And it's time for lunch."

☆   ☆   ☆

The Chez Toi is the best restaurant in the French Quarter. That's the upside of working for a major museum director.

"The curse made more sense," said Prang, after we had ordered. "Nobody sacrifices virgins to a robot."

"The Mayans didn't know from robots," I said. "Wasn't

it Arthur C. Clarke who said that any sufficiently advanced technology looks like magic?"

"That was Jules Verne," said Boudin. "But I must admit your theory fits the facts. According to Paris, the 'stone' is some kind of silicon substance with a toggling molecule that allows it to change from solid to flexible in an instant."

"Synthetique!" I said, digging into my chicken *provençale*.

"There's one big problem with your robot theory, or hunch, or whatever," said Prang. "The Enormé's half a million years old, remember?"

"Between 477,000 and 481,000," said Boudin, checking his scanner.

"So!" said Prang. She pushed her plate away and lit a Camel. "No one could have built a robot that long ago!"

"No one could have carved a statue either," Boudin pointed out. "No one on Earth, anyway."

"Exactly," I said.

"I'm afraid you can't smoke in here," said the waiter.

"Extraterrestrials?" said Prang, blowing a smoke ring shaped like a flying saucer. "Aliens? This is worse than ever. Now I need a science fiction private eye!"

"You had one all along," I said. "I never believed in the supernatural. I believe in the real world, and as Shakespeare said, "There are more things in Heaven and Earth than are dreamed of in our philosophy.""

"That was Voltaire," said Boudin. "But your point is well taken."

"You've both been watching too much *Star Tank*," said Prang, signing the check. "But whatever the Enormé is, I want to find it and get it back. Keep your phone on. What do you say we take a ride?"

The parking valet brought the big BMW around and gave up the keys with a visible sigh of regret.

"Where do we start?" Prang asked, as she peeled away from the curb (and I closed my eyes). "Any hunches?"

"None," I said. "I doubt the Enormé would hide in the cemeteries again, unless..."

"Unless it wanted to be found," said Boudin.

Prang's car phone rang.

"Prang here."

"Yes, find... Kill me..."

I lunged for the speaker phone switch. "Where are you? Are you awake?"

"No, dreaming..."

"Where are you?" asked Prang.

"City, city of the Dead..." He was fading. "Please kill me... before I wake..."

Click. Dial tone.

"City of the Dead. Big help!" Prang said. "New Orleans has over twenty cemeteries in the city limits alone!"

The car phone rang again.

"Prang here. Is that you, Enormé?"

"Keep your opinions to yourself," said Chief Ward. "Where are you, Prang? I hear your statue is gone missing again."

"I'm out for a drive, if it's any of your business," said Prang. "And don't worry about the statue. It's under control."

"We have ten calls from people who saw it walking up Rampart Street just before dawn. Prang what is this thing? A monster? Is it the murderer we're looking for?"

"Don't be silly, Ward. It's just a statue."

"We're putting out an all-points, shoot-to-kill."

"You can't do that! It's museum property."

"Stealing itself? What is this, Prang? Some sort of insurance scam?"

"Hang up!" Boudin whispered.

"Huh?"

"Boudin's right," I whispered. "Ward's using the car phone to track you!"

"Damn!" Prang hung up. "I thought he was awfully chatty!"

☆   ☆   ☆

We cruised the "Cities of the Dead" all afternoon, looking for opened gates. The GPS screen on the dash of the BMW allowed me to follow our progress without looking out the window and subjecting myself to the terrifying view of the pedestrians and cars Prang barely missed.

"You're sure that was it on the phone?" Prang asked. "Why would it want to be found?"

"I'm still working on that," I said. "It is activated by the moon, but only communicates when it's dormant. Perhaps we are stimulating some new response in it."

Boudin's scanner-communicator beeped.

"Anything new from Paris?" Prang asked, lighting a fresh Camel and pitching the old one out the window.

"Just filling out what we had," said Boudin, checking

the tiny screen. "The Enormé is solid all the way through. There is no internal anatomy at all, only field patterns in the pseudo stone activated by a tiny nuclear power cell buried in the center of the mass. The Enormé appears to have been grown, like a crystal, rather than made…"

"But who put it here?" Prang asked. "And why? There were no humans here half a million years ago. Just hominids, half human, hunting in packs."

"That's it!" I said. "Charlie's Angels!"

"Charlie who?" asked Boudin.

"Darwin. I've been having these weird dreams about Charles Darwin."

"Is this another hunch?" Prang asked.

"Maybe. Suppose you wanted to speed up evolution. How would you go about it?"

"Soup up the chromosones?" offered Prang, as she deftly maneuvered between an eastbound Coke and westbound Pepsi truck. I concentrated on the GPS screen again, where we were a flashing light.

"Make conditions harder," said Boudin. "Apply pressure."

"Exactly!" I said. "Suppose you found a species, a primate, for example, right on the verge of developing intelligence, language, culture. But it doesn't really need all that. It is perfectly capable of living in its ecological niche. It has intelligence, or at least enough; it makes fire; it even makes some crude tools—stone hammers, wooden spears. It has spread all over the planet and adapted to every environment, from the equator to the arctic. It is perfectly adapted to its environment."

"It's not going to evolve any farther," said Boudin.

"No reason to," I said. "Unless. Unless you seeded the planet with a killer—or killers. Killer robots. Berserkers that would pursue this species, relentlessly. Something that was big, fast, and hard to kill. And smart."

"Charlie's Angels," said Prang. "I get it. Survival of the fittest. Berserker robots with a mission: Evolve or else!"

The BMW's cell phone rang.

"If it's Ward don't let him keep you on the phone," I reminded Prang. "And if it's our friend..."

"Prang here. Hello?"

"You got it," said a deep, smoky, dreamlike voice. "Now kill me, please."

☆ ☆ ☆

"Got what?" Prang asked, as she scattered kids and crossing guards.

"Kill you?" I asked, eyes squeezed shut.

"So I can rest," said the Enormé over the car phone. "There were twelve of us. I am the last."

"Twelve what? Angels...I mean, robots?" The 740i has a speakerphone; I switched it on.

"One in each corner of your tear drop globe. We stalked and killed your kind, or what was then your kind. We slaughtered the weaklings and pushed the rest into the caves and cold hills. Out of the pretty plains. Away from the meat runs."

"The dragon myth," said Boudin. "Racial memory."

"There's no such thing as racial memory," said Prang.

"Nonsense," I told her. "What is culture but racial memory?"

"Then I slept for a thousand years. Dreaming. But I could not speak. Xomilcho could not hear. He would not kill me."

"Xomilcho?" Prang lit a fresh Camel. "Sounds like a chain store."

"Sounds Olmec to me," said Boudin. "Was Xomilcho the one who put you in the tomb?"

"Saved me from the moon. Let me dream and dream. But he would not kill me."

"We want to let you dream too," I said. "Where are you?"

"City of the Dead..."

"Which one?" Prang asked.

"C-c-city..."the Enormé began stuttering like a bad CD. "Can't t-t-tell w-which..."

Click.

"What happened?" asked Prang.

"We overloaded him," said Boudin. "If this berserker hunch is right, the Enormé is programmed to evade. He can't tell us where he is any more than we could decide not to breathe."

"Then we have to check them all, it's getting late!" said Prang, stepping on the gas. I didn't want to watch, so I ducked my head and watched the blinking light on the display. Our speed was alarming, even there.

Then I saw another blinking light, in the upper left hand corner of the screen. It was stationary.

"Head north," I said. "Crescent Street, near the corner of Citadelle."

"There are no cemeteries there," Prang protested. "Is this another hunch?"

"Yes!"

That was enough for her. I put my hands over my ears to block out the screaming of tires as she made a U-turn.

"Damn!" said Prang, as she power slid off Citadelle onto Crescent.

I opened my eyes just enough to see a run-down business district, with a Karate School, a Starbucks, a Woolworth's and an abandoned movie theater.

No cemeteries. Even though the street looked spooky enough in the gathering dusk. The sun was setting.

"A wild goose chase!" said Prang.

"Wait!" said Boudin. "Look what's playing."

I opened my eyes a little wider.

The marquee of the BIJOU was missing a few letters, but the title of the last feature was still readable:

CI Y OF HE DEAD.

We parked in front of Starbucks where the BMW wouldn't be so conspicuous. The BIJOU's wide front doors were chained shut, but I figured there would be an exit in the back, and I was right. I figured it would be smashed open—and I was right.

It was dark inside. The smells of old popcorn, tears, laughter, Cokes and kisses all mingled in a musty bouquet. The seats had all been torn out, sold (I supposed) to coffee shops or antique malls where they would seem quaint. The Enormé lay on the bare sloping concrete floor, his "eyes" staring straight up at the baroque ceiling with its cupids and curliques, angels and occasional gargoyle.

I approached and touched one great three-toed foot, like the first time. And like the first time, he was as cold as any stone. And I was glad he was cold, here, in the gloom, where he was safe from the rays of the rising moon.

"Cool!" whispered Prang. "Villon and his hunches! Give me your phone and I'll call the museum."

"Wait," I said. "Enormé might have something to say. He uses the phone to talk."

"I can dream here," said the familiar voice, booming through the theater. "I am safe here."

"Now he's coming through the speakers!" said Boudin. "Apparently he can access any electronic grid. Even turn it on. Even supply it with power."

"I am the last one," Enormé said. "They want you to kill me."

"Who?" I asked. "Who made you?"

"The Makers. Made us to make you. Sailed the stars and found the little tear-drop worlds where life could be nudged awake. Yours was not called Earth then. It was not called anything. Your kind was all over the planet, silent but strong."

"Strong?" Prang said. "We were weak."

"That's a myth," said Boudin. "Actually, Homo was the most impressive killer on the planet, even without language and culture. With fire and hands, sticks and stones, hunting in packs, he could live anywhere and face down even the saber tooth."

"Yes," Enormé's voice boomed. "You were the king of the beasts. We made you something more."

"Made us?" Prang asked.

"To survive, you had to kill us. To kill us you had to develop tools, cooperation, language. Understanding. Kill us one by one. We were hunted, with sticks, with stones. Smashed with boulders, thrown into fiery pits, buried alive. There was no dreaming in that dance. I am the last."

"How come we never found the others?" Prang asked, lighting the Camel in her mouth off the one in her hand.

"Maybe we did," I said. I was thinking of statues in Greece, India, the Middle East. But Enormé corrected me:

"All that is solid melts into air. Killed we are set free. Back to nothingness. It is the end of our pain. And of our usefulness."

"You don't mind dying, then?" asked Prang.

"No. Killing is what we do. What I do. Dying is what we are. What I am."

"We don't want to kill you," I said. "We want to let you dream."

"Xomilcho let me sleep. He kept me away from the pearl world that awakens me. He let me sleep the centuries. Then, a hundred years ago I began to dream."

"He must mean radio!" said Boudin. "As soon as there was an electronic grid on the planet, it awakened something in him."

"I can only dream when I am not awake. I have been dreaming for a hundred years. You awakened me so that I could barely dream."

"That was our mistake," said Prang. "We will let you sleep. We'll build a special room for you in the museum, and you can dream forever."

"They want you to kill me," said Enormé. "They want to come."

"Cool," said Prang. "They can come too."

I felt a chill. "Don't be so sure. We don't know what they are. Or what they want."

"When we are killed, it is done," Enormé said. "The Makers will come."

"He's a transmitter!" Boudin said. "When he dies, they will know we have survived. He's a trigger, a signal."

"Or an alarm," I said. "If we kill him they know we have evolved. But they will also know we didn't evolve past killing."

"What are you saying?" Boudin asked.

"Maybe we're not supposed to kill the last one. Maybe it's a test."

"Is that another hunch?" asked Prang.

"Maybe it's not our decision to make, since it involves the whole world."

"They want you to kill me," Enormé repeated, his voice echoing through the theater. "The Makers will come down from the sky. It will be over."

"Forget about dying!" said Prang. She pointed at her watch, then at Boudin and me. "Let's leave him here in the dark till morning. Then we have to get Enormé back to the museum and out of harm's way before the police find him. Otherwise..."

"Too late," said Boudin, looking up. I could hear the whump-whump-whump of a chopper hovering overhead.

☆　☆　☆

"Damn!" said Prang. "Just when..."

The helicopter drowned out her voice. Boudin and I looked at each other helplessly. We heard footsteps on the roof, on the fire escape; we heard sirens outside.

CRASH! Suddenly the stage door burst open. "Stand back! Hostages, stand back."

"Ward!" I cried. "We're not hostages! Don't shoot. We just discovered what this thing is. It's..."

"I know what it is, it's a monster!" said Ward, stepping in front of his troops with a bullhorn. "I've got the place surrounded!"

And he did. The front door burst open and armed cops appeared. They all wore flak jackets. Two carried anti-tank guns.

"Don't shoot!" Prang said, stepping coolly into the line of fire. "Ward, I can explain everything!"

"This had better not be a trick!" Ward shouted.

"No trick!" said Prang. "It's a federal matter. Hell, it's international. And we need your help, Chief Ward!"

It was the "Chief" that did it. "Hold your fire, men!" Ward shouted. The SWAT cops lowered their weapons.

"Close call!" I whispered to Boudin, as Prang took Ward's arm and pulled him aside. She spoke fast, in low tones, pointing first at the Enormé, then at the ceiling, then back at the Enormé.

Ward looked puzzled, then skeptical, then amazed. Boudin smiled at me, and we breathed a collective sigh of relief.

Too soon.

Behind Ward and Prang, through the smashed-open rear exit, I could see a vacant lot and bare trees, outlined against the rising moon. The silver light washed across the concrete floor like spilled paint.

"Ward! Prang! Close the door!" I shouted.

Too late. I heard a groan behind me.

"No!" I heard my own voice shouting, as Enormé stood up. The saucer eyes were shining; a voice boomed over the theater speakers: "Kill me..."

TAT TAT TAT!

BLAM BLAM!

Bullets whined as they ricocheted off the pseudo stone. Enormé spun around and around in a grotesque dance, his wide eyes pleading, his stubby arms reaching out, for the door, for the moon...

"Hold your fire!" I yelled.

KA-BLAM!

The theater rocked with the blast of an anti-tank shell. Enormé spun one last time—then shattered, and fell to the concrete floor in pieces.

"No!" I yelled, stumbling, falling to my knees.

It was all over.

Prang and Ward edged closer and closer to the shapeless pile of pseudo stone. Boudin helped me up, and I joined them.

"What the hell..." Ward muttered. The pieces were starting to smoke, like dry ice. The Enormé was fading: all that is solid melts into air. We watched in astonished silence until the pieces all were gone, as if he had never been.

"What the hell was that, a ghost?" asked Ward, looking at me almost with respect.

I shook my head and retreated to the open door. I couldn't answer him. I couldn't bear to look at him.

"That was a robot!" said Prang, angrily extracting the last Camel from her pack. "From outer space. And priceless, you idiot!"

"Sent here half a million years ago to accelerate our evolution," Boudin explained. "And to signal its Makers when we were finally capable of destroying it."

"Well, it's sure as hell destroyed," said Ward. "So I guess we sure as hell passed the test."

"No, you fool." I stepped outside, past the puzzled cops, and looked up at the brilliant cold full moon, and beyond it, a few faraway stars, scattered like broken glass across the dark floor of the universe.

I wished I had a cigarette. I wondered what the Makers were and what they would do with us when they came.

"No," I said again, to no one in particular, "I think we flunked."

Author's Afterword

I feel bad, but only a little, about my Epistolary Epic "Pirates of the Somali Coast": the actual Somali pirates are never so cruel! Originally published by Ellen Datlow in *Subterranean* magazine, it made Hartwell's *Year's Best SF*. So did the deliberately retro "Brother, Can You Spare a Dime," which was written for *Yesterday's Tomorrows: The Golden Age of SF*.

The rigorously Noir "Charlie's Angels," also a Datlow (SciFiction) and Hartwell pick, had a grievous astronomical error in its original incarnation which has been, also rigorously, corrected.

"Catch 'Em in the Act," my first and only Little Shop story, was bought by Patrick Nielsen Hayden for *www.Tor.com*. So was the rather more controversial "TVA Baby." Just for the record, a TVA baby is a Southerner whose Yankee father came down to work for Roosevelt's Tennessee Valley Authority.

"Farewell Atlantis," my first and only Generation Ship story, was published in *Fantasy & Science Fiction* at precisely moment that a hoax novel with the same title showed up on the internet promoting the disastrous disaster movie *2012*.

Coincidence? Ask the Mayans. Or was it the Aztecs?

"Private Eye" was written for *Playboy*, the traditional home for my Romantic Comedies. Alas, they passed, and Gordon Van Gelder picked it up for *F&SF*.

"BYOB FAQ" was published in *Nature* magazine's series of SF short shorts; they didn't want "CORONA

CENTURION™ FAQ" but Gordon came to the rescue again. It has already been overtaken by reality: Dick Cheney actually has such a heart!

"Captain Ordinary" was intended for Geoff Ryman's special "mundane" issue of *Interzone*, illustrating his contrarian argument that SF should eschew faster-than-light travel, telepathy, superhero mutants, and the like, and dramatize more likely (mundane) futures. Geoff wasn't amused, but Rudy Rucker liked it for his prestigious online e-zine *Flurb*.

"Billy and the Circus Girl," is the only Billy story *not* included in my recent *Billy's Book* collection. It's not for kids. Except for Rudy, who took it for *Flurb*.

"A Special Day" was commissioned by *New York Magazine* for their 9/11 fifth anniversary issue (2006). They turned it down as "too sentimental," a first for me. I spent the kill fee on six-year-old bourbon and ran it on *Amazon Shorts* instead.

"The Stamp," my shortest short-short ever, was written for *Boy's Life* but published online in *Lone Star Stories* instead. There will always be a Texas.

This is my fourth collection, and my first for PM. You will notice that several of the stories in this batch were rejected and then rescued. In California used-car parlance they would be called "salvage titles." They still start and run, though, at least for me.

I hope they work for you as well.

Terry Bisson, who was for many years a Kentuckian living in New York City, is now a New Yorker living in California. In addition to his Hugo and Nebula award winning science fiction, Bisson has written children's books, comics, screenplays and biographies of John Brown, Nat Turner, and Mumia Abu-Jamal.

He is also the host of a popular San Francisco reading series (SFinSF) and the Editor of PM's Outspoken Authors pocketbook series.

He lives in Oakland and rides a KLR650.

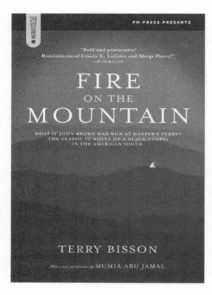

PM PRESS SPECTACULAR FICTION

Fire on the Mountain
Terry Bisson
978-1-60486-087-0
$15.95

It's 1959 in socialist Virginia. The Deep South is an independent Black nation called Nova Africa. The second Mars expedition is about to touch down on the red planet. And a pregnant scientist is climbing the Blue Ridge in search of her great-great grandfather, a teenage slave who fought with John Brown and Harriet Tubman's guerrilla army.

Long unavailable in the U.S., published in France as *Nova Africa*, *Fire on the Mountain* is the story of what might have happened if John Brown's raid on Harper's Ferry had succeeded—and the Civil War had been started not by the slave owners but the abolitionists.

About the Author:
Terry Bisson, who was for many years a Kentuckian living in New York City, is now a New Yorker living in California. In addition to science fiction, he has written bios of Mumia Abu-Jamal and Nat Turner. He is also the host of a popular San Francisco reading series (SFinSF) and the Editor of PM's new Outspoken Authors pocketbook series.

"Few works have moved me as deeply, as thoroughly, as Terry Bisson's *Fire On The Mountain*… With this single poignant story, Bisson molds a world as sweet as banana cream pies, and as briny as hot tears."
—Mumia Abu-Jamal, death row prisoner and author of *Live From Death Row*, from the Introduction.

PM PRESS
OUTSPOKEN AUTHORS

Mammoths of the
Great Plains
Eleanor Arnason
978-1-60486-075-7
$12

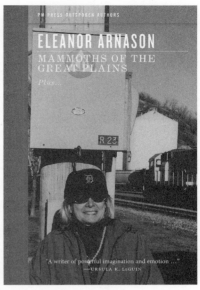

When President Thomas Jefferson sent Lewis and Clark to explore the West, he told them to look especially for mammoths. Jefferson had seen bones and tusks of the great beasts in Virginia, and he suspected—he hoped!—that they might still roam the Great Plains. In Eleanor Arnason's imaginative alternate history, they do: shaggy herds thunder over the grasslands, living symbols of the oncoming struggle between the Native peoples and the European invaders. And in an unforgettable saga that soars from the badlands of the Dakotas to the icy wastes of Siberia, from the Russian Revolution to the AIM protests of the 1960s, Arnason tells of a modern woman's struggle to use the weapons of DNA science to fulfill the ancient promises of her Lakota heritage.

PLUS: "Writing SF During World War III," and an Outspoken Interview that takes you straight into the heart and mind of one of today's edgiest and most uncompromising speculative authors.

About the Author:
Ever since her first story was published in the revolutionary *New Worlds* in 1972, Eleanor Arnason has been acknowledged as the heir to the feminist legacy of Russ and Le Guin. The first winner of the prestigious Tiptree Award, she has been short listed for both the Nebula and the Hugo.

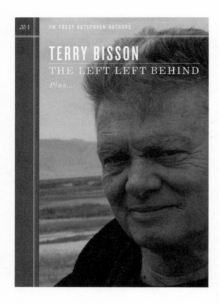

PM PRESS
OUTSPOKEN AUTHORS

The Left *Left Behind*
Terry Bisson
978-1-60486-086-3
$12

Hugo and Nebula award-win-
ner Terry Bisson is best known
for his short stories, which
range from the southern
sweetness of "Bears Discover
Fire" to the alienated aliens of
"They're Made out of Meat."
He is also a 1960s' New Left
vet with a history of activism
and an intact (if battered) radical ideology.

The *Left Behind* novels (about the so-called "Rapture" in which
all the born-agains ascend straight to heaven) are among the bestselling Christian books in the U.S., describing in lurid detail the
adventures of those "left behind" to battle the Anti-Christ. Put
Bisson and the Born-Agains together, and what do you get? *The*
Left *Left Behind*-a sardonic, merciless, tasteless, take-no-prisoners satire of the entire apocalyptic enterprise that spares no one-
predatory preachers, goth lingerie, Pacifica radio, Indian casinos,
gangsta rap, and even "art cars" at Burning Man.

Plus: "Special Relativity," a one-act drama that answers the question: When Albert Einstein, Paul Robeson, J. Edgar Hoover are
raised from the dead at an anti-Bush rally, which one wears the
dress? As with all Outspoken Author books, there is a deep interview and autobiography: at length, in-depth, no-holds-barred
and all-bets off: an extended tour though the mind and work,
the history and politics of our Outspoken Author. Surprises are
promised.

PM PRESS
OUTSPOKEN AUTHORS

The Lucky Strike
Kim Stanley Robinson
978-1-60486-085-6
$12

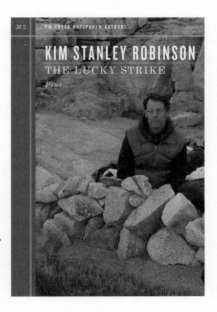

Combining dazzling specula-
tion with a profoundly humanist vision, Kim Stanley Robinson is known as not only the
most literary but also the most
progressive (read "radical") of
today's top rank SF authors.
His bestselling "Mars Trilogy"
tells the epic story of the future
colonization of the red planet,
and the revolution that inevitably follows. His latest novel, *Galileo's
Dream*, is a stunning combination of historical drama and far-flung
space opera, in which the ten dimensions of the universe itself are
rewoven to ensnare history's most notorious torturers.

The Lucky Strike, the classic and controversial story Robinson has
chosen for PM's new Outspoken Authors series, begins on a lonely
Pacific island, where a crew of untested men are about to take off
in an untried aircraft with a deadly payload that will change our
world forever. Until something goes wonderfully wrong.

Plus: *A Sensitive Dependence on Initial Conditions*, in which Robinson dramatically deconstructs "alternate history" to explore what
might have been if things had gone differently over Hiroshima that
day.

As with all Outspoken Author books, there is a deep interview and
autobiography: at length, in-depth, no-holds-barred and all-bets
off: an extended tour though the mind and work, the history and
politics of our Outspoken Author.

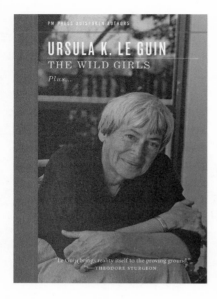

PM PRESS
OUTSPOKEN AUTHORS

The Wild Girls
Ursula K. Le Guin
978-1-60486-403-8
$12

Ursula K. Le Guin is the one modern science fiction author who truly needs no introduction. In the forty years since *The Left Hand of Darkness*, her works have changed not only the face but the tone and the agenda of SF, introducing themes of gender, race, socialism and anarchism, all the while thrilling readers with trips to strange (and strangely familiar) new worlds. She is our exemplar of what fantastic literature can and should be about.

Her Nebula winner *The Wild Girls*, newly revised and presented here in book form for the first time, tells of two captive "dirt children" in a society of sword and silk, whose determination to enter "that possible even when unattainable space in which there is room for justice" leads to a violent and loving end.

Plus: Le Guin's scandalous and scorching *Harper's* essay, "Staying Awake While We Read", (also collected here for the first time) which demolishes the pretensions of corporate publishing and the basic assumptions of capitalism as well. And of course our Outspoken Interview which promises to reveal the hidden dimensions of America's best-known SF author. And delivers.

"If you want excess and risk and intelligence, try Le Guin."
—*The San Francisco Chronicle*

PM PRESS
OUTSPOKEN AUTHORS

Modem Times 2.0
Michael Moorcock
978-1-60486-308-6
$12

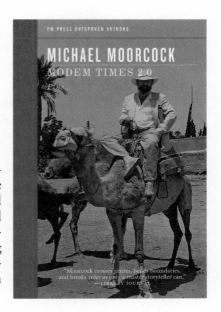

As the editor of London's revolutionary *New Worlds* magazine in the swinging sixties, Michael Moorcock has been credited with virtually inventing modern Science Fiction: publishing such figures as Norman Spinrad, Samuel R. Delany, Brian Aldiss and J.G. Ballard.

Moorcock's own literary accomplishments include his classic *Mother London*, a romp through urban history conducted by psychic outsiders; his comic *Pyat* quartet, in which a Jewish antisemite examines the roots of the Nazi Holocaust; *Behold The Man*, the tale of a time tourist who fills in for Christ on the cross; and of course the eternal hero Elric, swordswinger, hellbringer and bestseller.

And now Moorcock's most audacious creation, Jerry Cornelius—assassin, rock star, chronospy and maybe-Messiah--is back in *Modem Times 2.0*, a time twisting odyssey that connects 60s London with post-Obama America, with stops in Palm Springs and Guantanamo. *Modem Times 2.0* is Moorcock at his most outrageously readable--a masterful mix of erudition and subversion.

Plus: a non-fiction romp in the spirit of Swift and Orwell, Fields of Folly; and an Outspoken Interview with literature's authentic Lord of Misrule.

PM PRESS
FOUND IN TRANSLATION

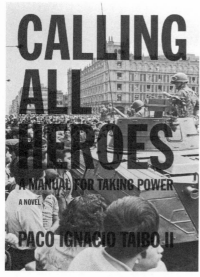

Calling All Heroes:
A Manual for Taking Power
Paco Ignacio Taibo II
Translated by Gregory Nipper
978-1-60486-205-8
$12

The euphoric idealism of grassroots reform and the tragic reality of revolutionary failure are at the center of this speculative novel that opens with a real historical event. On October 2, 1968, 10 days before the Summer Olympics in Mexico, the Mexican government responds to a student demonstration in Tlatelolco by firing into the crowd, killing more than 200 students and civilians and wounding hundreds more. The massacre of Tlatelolco was erased from the official record as easily as authorities washing the blood from the streets, and no one was ever held accountable.

It is two years later and Nestor, a journalist and participant in the fateful events, lies recovering in the hospital from a knife wound. His fevered imagination leads him in the collection of facts and memories of the movement and its assassination in the company of figures from his childhood. Nestor calls on the heroes of his youth—Sherlock Holmes, Doc Holliday, Wyatt Earp and D'Artagnan among them—to join him in launching a new reform movement conceived by his intensely active imagination.

"The real enchantment of Mr. Taibo's storytelling lies in the wild and melancholy tangle of life he sees everywhere."
—*New York Times Book Review*

PM PRESS
OUTSPOKEN AUTHORS

The Underbelly
Gary Phillips
978-1-60486-206-5
$14

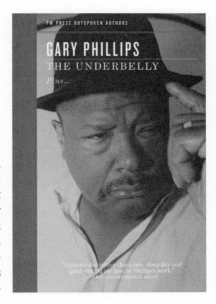

The explosion of wealth and development in downtown L.A. is a thing of wonder. But regardless of how big and shiny our buildings get, we should not forget the ones this wealth and development has overlooked and pushed out. This is the context for Phillips' novella *The Underbelly*, as a semi-homeless Vietnam vet named Magrady searches for a wheelchair-bound friend gone missing from Skid Row—a friend who might be working a dangerous scheme against major players. Magrady's journey is a solo sortie where the flashback-prone protagonist must deal with the impact of gentrification; take-no-prisoners community organizers; an unflinching cop from his past in Vietnam; an elderly sexpot out for his bones; a lusted-after magical skull; chronic-lovin' knuckleheads; and the perils of chili cheese fries at midnight. Combining action, humor and a street level gritty POV, *The Underbelly* is illustrated with photos and drawings.

Plus: a rollicking interview wherein Phillips riffs on Ghetto Lit, politics, noir and the proletariat, the good negroes and bad knee-grows of pop culture, Redd Foxx and Lord Buckley, and wrestles with the future of books in the age of want.

"Magrady's adventures, with a distinctive noir feeling and appreciation for comic books, started as an online, serialized mystery. Drawings and an interview with Phillips enhance the package, offering a compelling perspective on race and class issues in South Central L.A." —*Booklist*

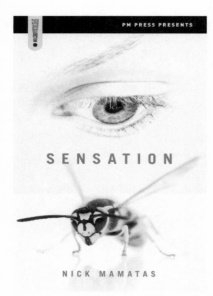

SENSATION

NICK MAMATAS

PM PRESS
SPECTACULAR FICTION

Sensation
Nick Mamatas
978-1-60486-084-9
$14.95

Love. Politics. Parasitic manipula-
tion. Julia Hernandez left her husband, shot a real-estate developer
out to gentrify Brooklyn, and then
vanished without a trace. Well, perhaps one or two traces were left...
With different personal and con-
sumption habits, Julia has slipped
out of the world she knew and into
the Simulacrum—a place between
the cracks of our existence from
which human history is both guided and thwarted by the conflict between
a species of anarchist wasp and a collective of hyperintelligent spider. When
Julia's ex-husband Raymond spots her in a grocery store he doesn't usually
patronize, he's drawn into an underworld of radical political gestures and
Internet organizing looking to overthrow a ruling class it knows nothing
about—and Julia is the new media sensation of both this world and the
Simulacrum.

Told ultimately from the collective point of view of another species, *Sensation*
plays with the elements of the Simulacrum we all already live in: media
reports, businessspeak, blog entries, text messages, psychological evaluation
forms, and the always fraught and kindly lies lovers tell one another.

About the Author:
Nick Mamatas is the author of three novels, including *Move Under Ground*
and *Under My Roof*, which have been translated into German, Italian, and
Greek and nominated for the Bram Stoker and International Horror Guild
awards and the Kurd Lasswitz Prize. Many of his sixty short stories were
recently collected in *You Might Sleep...* As co-editor of *Clarkesworld*, the
online magazine of the fantastic, he was nominated for the World Fantasy
award and for science fiction's Hugo award, and with Ellen Datlow he is
co-editor of the anthology *Haunted Legends*. Nick's reportage and essays on
radical politics, digital society, pop culture and everyday life have appeared in
the *Village Voice*, *In These Times*, *Clamor*, *The New Humanist*, *The Smart Set*
and many other venues, including various Disinformation and Smart Pop
Books anthologies. A native New Yorker, Nick now lives in the California
Bay Area.

PM Press was founded at the end of 2007 by a small collection of folks with decades of publishing, media, and organizing experience. PM Press co-conspirators have published and distributed hundreds of books, pamphlets, CDs, and DVDs. Members of PM have founded enduring book fairs, spearheaded victorious tenant organizing campaigns, and worked closely with bookstores, academic conferences, and even rock bands to deliver political and challenging ideas to all walks of life. We're old enough to know what we're doing and young enough to know what's at stake.

We seek to create radical and stimulating fiction and non-fiction books, pamphlets, t-shirts, visual and audio materials to entertain, educate, and inspire you. We aim to distribute these through every available channel with every available technology, whether that means you are seeing anarchist classics at our bookfair stalls; reading our latest vegan cookbook at the café; downloading geeky fiction e-books; or digging new music and timely videos from our website.

PM Press is always on the lookout for talented and skilled volunteers, artists, activists and writers to work with. If you have a great idea for a project or can contribute in some way, please get in touch.

PM Press
PO Box 23912
Oakland CA 94623
510-658-3906
www.pmpress.org

FRIENDS OF

These are indisputably momentous times – the financial system is melting down globally and the Empire is stumbling. Now more than ever there is a vital need for radical ideas.

In the three years since its founding – and on a mere shoestring – PM Press has risen to the formidable challenge of publishing and distributing knowledge and entertainment for the struggles ahead. With over 100 releases to date, we have published an impressive and stimulating array of literature, art, music, politics, and culture. Using every available medium, we've succeeded in connecting those hungry for ideas and information to those putting them into practice.

Friends of PM allows you to directly help impact, amplify, and revitalize the discourse and actions of radical writers, filmmakers, and artists. It provides us with a stable foundation from which we can build upon our early successes and provides a much-needed subsidy for the materials that can't necessarily pay their own way. You can help make that happen – and receive every new title automatically delivered to your door once a month – by joining as a Friend of PM Press. And, we'll throw in a free T-Shirt when you sign up.

Here are your options:

- $25 a month: Get all books and pamphlets plus 50% discount on all webstore purchases
- $25 a month: Get all CDs and DVDs plus 50% discount on all webstore purchases
- $40 a month: Get all PM Press releases plus 50% discount on all webstore purchases
- $100 a month: Superstar - Everything plus PM merchandise, free downloads, and 50% discount on all webstore purchases

For those who can't afford $25 or more a month, we're introducing **Sustainer Rates** at $15, $10 and $5. Sustainers get a free PM Press t-shirt and a 50% discount on all purchases from our website.

Your Visa or Mastercard will be billed once a month, until you tell us to stop. Or until our efforts succeed in bringing the revolution around. Or the financial meltdown of Capital makes plastic redundant. Whichever comes first.